A Collect wonderful book of short stories woven from the wonderful mind of Cal Sherwood with special help and consideration from Stephanie Wood, G.B. Malone, Sarrah Keyes and Yvonne DeSander. I know that Short Stories in general is a very specific genre, so I thank you, all of you readers, for your support.

Lightning In a Bottle

Awake At a Wake

Dukes Opus

Going Up

Lightning In a Bottle

By Cal Sherwood

These short stories are a work of fiction. Unless otherwise indicated, all the names, characters, businesses, places, events and incidents in this book are either the product of the author's imagination or used in a fictitious manner. Any resemblance to actual persons, living or dead, or actual events is purely coincidental.

Chapter One: Sparks Ignite

Windhaven Academy loomed over the manicured landscape like a fortress of privilege, its ivy-covered walls concealing the secrets of the elite. Selma sauntered through the grand entrance, her steps echoing defiance in the hallowed halls. Dressed in a leather jacket that whispered rebellion and confidence, she was the embodiment of teenage insubordination.

Her destination: Room 214, the lair of Mr. Donovan Sterling, the enigmatic Creative Writing tutor hired by her parents to sculpt her unruly creativity. Selma's eyes sparkled with mischief as she pushed open the door, the heavy oak protesting her intrusion.

The room smelled of aged paper and possibility, the walls adorned with literary masterpieces that seemed to mock the confines of academia. Mr. Sterling sat behind a mahogany desk, his piercing gaze gliding up from the worn manuscript he was perusing.

"Miss Selma," he greeted, a wry smile playing on his lips. "What brings you to my domain?"

She grinned, all sharp edges and confidence. "I was hoping for a private lesson, Mr. Sterling. Your classes are electrifying, and I want to explore the depths of creativity you seem so adept at unlocking."

He chuckled, a sound that resonated in the room like a prelude to something dangerous. "Creativity is a wild beast, Selma. Are you ready to tame it?"

Thus began their clandestine dance, an intricate choreography of intellect and desire. Selma's rebellious spirit collided with Mr. Sterling's erudition, creating sparks that ignited the air between them. Every stolen glance, every shared secret, added a layer to the magnetic force that bound them.

Days turned into weeks, and their forbidden connection deepened. The classroom became a haven where words became an unspoken language of longing. Selma's writing, once an untamed beast, now bore the mark of Mr. Sterling's influence – a dance of seduction and poetry.

One rainy afternoon, Selma entered his office with a look that betrayed the storm within. "Mr. Sterling, let's stop playing with metaphors and dive into the real story."

His gaze met hers, a storm of conflict brewing in his eyes. "Selma, we're treading on dangerous ground. I'm your teacher."

She approached, her movements a sultry ballet.

"Sometimes, the best stories are written on forbidden pages, don't you think?"

Their lips met in a collision of hunger and rebellion, sealing a pact that would forever alter the course of their narratives. As the rain outside intensified, their love story unfolded, chapter by chapter, in the dimly lit corners of Windhaven Academy, where the lightning they had captured in their bottle threatened to illuminate the shadows of their clandestine passion.

Chapter Two: Whispers in the Shadows

The rain outside tapped a clandestine rhythm on the windowpanes as Selma reclined in the worn leather chair across from Mr. Sterling's desk. The air hung heavy with anticipation, a symphony of unspoken desires enveloping them like a fog.

Mr. Sterling, his dark eyes filled with both longing and trepidation, broke the silence. "Selma, we're traversing a precarious path. This affair, it's like dancing on the edge of a storm. We're playing with fire."

She met his gaze with a knowing smile, her green eyes aflame with rebellion. "But isn't that where the most magnificent flames are born, Mr. Sterling? In the heart of the tempest?"

He sighed, the weight of responsibility heavy on his shoulders. "You're of age, Selma, but the dynamics of teacher and student create a web of complications. Our affair could unravel everything we hold dear."

Selma leaned forward, her voice a sultry murmur. "Then let it unravel, Mr. Sterling. Isn't that what creativity is all about? Breaking free from the constraints of convention?"

Their conversation danced between the lines of propriety, a poetic code that only they could decipher. Mr. Sterling, caught in the intricate web of Selma's words, couldn't deny the allure of her metaphorical dance.

"Selma," he began, his tone a blend of caution and yearning, "our connection is like a novel written in invisible ink. A masterpiece hidden in plain sight, waiting to be discovered."

She chuckled, a sound that echoed through the room like the prelude to a forbidden sonnet. "Ah, Mr. Sterling, we are architects of a secret cathedral, constructing our love in the shadows where no one dares to look."

As the rain outside intensified, their words painted a canvas of longing and clandestine passion. Selma, drop-dead gorgeous and untamed, reveled in the forbidden dance. Mr. Sterling, caught in the whirlwind of her allure, succumbed to the intoxicating poetry of their illicit affair.

"Mr. Sterling," she whispered, her breath a sultry caress against his ear, "let our love be a story etched in the margins of society, where only the daring venture."

He traced a finger along the edge of her jaw, his touch a whisper of surrender. "Selma, our love is a sonnet written in the ink of rebellion, each stanza a testament to the danger we embrace."

In that dimly lit room, where shadows embraced secrets, Selma and Mr. Sterling forged a narrative that defied the conventional rules of love. The lightning in their bottle illuminated the clandestine corners of their desires, and as they embraced the storm, they wondered if, in the end, the tempest would be their salvation or their undoing.

Chapter Three: The Quill's Challenge

The air in Mr. Sterling's office held the lingering scent of their forbidden rendezvous as Selma settled into the leather chair. The rain outside continued its rhythmic serenade, a backdrop to the clandestine symphony unfolding between them.

Mr. Sterling, his eyes a reflection of the storm within, regarded Selma with a mixture of admiration and concern. "Selma, our affair is like a novel with chapters untold. But let us transcend the ephemeral and delve into the realm of creation. I have a challenge for you."

She arched an eyebrow, her interest piqued. "A challenge, Mr. Sterling? I'm all ears."

He leaned forward, his gaze intense. "Write for me, Selma, in the style of your favorite author. Channel the essence of their prose and craft something magnificent, something that will echo in the corridors of literary history."

A sly smile graced Selma's lips. "And who might this favorite author of mine be?"

Mr. Sterling's eyes gleamed with mischief. "You've mentioned Fitzgerald more than once. Imagine, Selma, if F. Scott himself were whispering in your ear, guiding your pen."

She chuckled; the challenge accepted. "Very well, Mr. Sterling. Challenge accepted. I'll channel the spirit of Fitzgerald and write a story that will set the literary world ablaze."

Days turned into nights as Selma immersed herself in the world of Gatsby-esque glamour and melancholy. The tap of rain on the windowpane served as her muse, guiding her pen as it danced across the pages. In those solitary moments, she wove a narrative that mirrored the intensity of their clandestine love – a tale of passion, rebellion, and the intoxicating allure of the forbidden.

With the manuscript complete, Selma handed it to Mr. Sterling, a glint of anticipation in her eyes. "Here it is, Mr. Sterling. A story born from the ashes of our forbidden dance."

He read with a furrowed brow, the words a revelation that mirrored the tempest they had embraced. As he finished, he looked at Selma with a mixture of awe and pride. "Selma, this is magnificent. You've captured the essence of Fitzgerald with a touch of your own brilliance."

An idea sparked in Mr. Sterling's mind, a daring plan to set their love story on a broader stage. "I'm entering this into a writing contest. Your words deserve to be heard, to echo beyond the confines of our secret world."

Selma's eyes widened, a mix of excitement and trepidation. "A writing contest? What if someone discovers our story?"

Mr. Sterling took her hands in his, the connection between them undeniable. "Let them discover, Selma. Our love, like your words, deserves to be recognized. Let the world marvel at the lightning we've bottled."

As the rain outside continued its passionate dance, Selma and Mr. Sterling braced themselves for the storm their words would unleash upon the literary world. The quill's challenge had been met, and the pages of their clandestine affair were about to be written in the annals of history, a narrative that defied convention and embraced the electric symphony of their forbidden love.

Chapter Four: Whispers of Triumph and Envy

The announcement of the writing contest results echoed through the hallowed halls of Windhaven Academy. Selma, with her tale of decadence and rebellion, emerged victorious, her words capturing the judges' hearts and leaving an indelible mark on the literary landscape.

Mr. Sterling, torn between pride and a pang of jealousy, had also submitted his own creation, a narrative that paled in comparison to Selma's brilliance. He congratulated her, his eyes a tempest of conflicting emotions.

"Selma," he began, "your victory is well-deserved. Your words are a revelation, a testament to the untamed spirit that resides within you."

She smiled, radiant in her triumph. "Mr. Sterling, perhaps you were the muse I needed to unlock the depths of my creativity."

Yet, as the accolades rained down on Selma, a major publishing house caught wind of her groundbreaking story. The whisper of her triumph reached the ears of a literary agent, and soon, the doors of opportunity swung wide open for the drop-dead gorgeous rebel.

In Mr. Sterling's eyes, a mixture of pride and jealousy battled for dominance. He, too, was a wordsmith, a maestro of storytelling, and yet, his creation had not garnered the attention that Selma's had.

"Selma," he confessed, his voice a murmur in the shadows, "your talent is undeniable. But in this moment, I find myself torn between pride in your achievement and a twinge of envy."

She approached, her gaze a storm of understanding. "Mr. Sterling, our stories may be different, but isn't the beauty of literature found in its diversity? Your time will come, and when it does, I'll be cheering you on."

As Selma's literary star ascended, Mr. Sterling grappled with the complexities of their shared narrative. The lightning in their bottle had sparked a fire that illuminated not only their forbidden connection but also the diverging paths their literary destinies would take.

And so, the echoes of Selma's triumph reverberated through the halls, leaving a tale of envy, pride, and the undeniable allure of a rebellious spirit in its wake.

Chapter Five: A Rising Star

Selma's literary triumph didn't merely stop at the writing contest victory. The whisper of her mesmerizing tale reached the ears of a prominent publishing house, eager to embrace the brilliance of a new and daring voice. Offers poured in, and soon, Selma found herself signing a contract with one of the most prestigious publishers in the literary world.

News of her ascent echoed through the ivory towers of Windhaven Academy, and the administration took notice. Mr. Sterling, the enigmatic tutor whose guidance had nurtured Selma's creativity, found himself not only celebrated but also rewarded. A raise, they said, for being the muse behind a soon-to-be best-selling author.

In the midst of this triumph, Selma and Mr. Sterling continued their clandestine dance, their connection now tinged with the glamour of success. Their meetings in the dimly lit corners of Windhaven Academy became moments of celebration, each stolen glance a reflection of the electric charge between them.

One afternoon, as they reveled in the warmth of their shared triumph, a knock on Mr. Sterling's office door disrupted their cocoon of secrecy. Panicked, they straightened their disheveled appearance just as the door creaked open.

A male student, oblivious to the complexity of their connection, entered with a sheepish smile. "Mr. Sterling, I was hoping to discuss my last assignment."

As Mr. Sterling provided guidance, Selma's eyes caught the glint of understanding in the student's gaze. The air thickened with unspoken tension, and as the young man left, Selma's heart raced with the realization that their secret was perilously close to being exposed.

Later, in the quiet sanctuary of Mr. Sterling's office, Selma grappled with the near-miss. "Mr. Sterling, we're walking on a tightrope. How long can we keep this hidden?"

He sighed, the weight of their forbidden connection pressing upon him. "Selma, our story is like a meteor streaking through the sky—bright, dazzling, but destined to burn out. We must be cautious."

Their moment of reflection was interrupted by another unexpected visitor. This time, it was the young student who had almost stumbled upon their secret. He hesitated, his eyes betraying a storm of conflicting emotions.

"Selma," he confessed, his voice laced with vulnerability, "I can't help but feel something when I see you and Mr. Sterling together. I... I think I'm in love with you."

Selma's gaze met Mr. Sterling's, and in that charged silence, the complexities of their forbidden connection unfolded. The student's confession hung in the air like an unanswered question, a collision of emotions threatening to unravel the delicate threads of their clandestine affair.

As Selma navigated the tumultuous waters of newfound success and tangled emotions, the winds of change swept through Windhaven

Academy, carrying with them the promise of revelation and transformation.

Chapter Six: Sculpted Obsession

The air in Windhaven Academy became charged with an unsettling energy as Selma's classmate, the one who had confessed his infatuation, tiptoed on the edge of obsession. Unbeknownst to her, he embarked on a peculiar artistic endeavor—a soap sculpture that aimed to immortalize her in a state of undress.

Whispers circulated through the hallowed halls, hinting at the illicit creation that bordered on voyeurism. Selma, busy preparing for the release of her upcoming novel "Lightning in a

Bottle," remained oblivious to the growing storm of fascination surrounding her.

One fateful day, as the sun dipped below the horizon, casting long shadows through Windhaven Academy, a mysterious package arrived at Selma's doorstep. The unwrapping revealed a soap sculpture—a nude bust of herself, intricately carved with an unsettling blend of infatuation and artistic skill.

A chill crawled up Selma's spine as her eyes scanned the contours of the sculpture. She felt exposed, as if her very essence had been laid bare for someone else's voyeuristic pleasure. The nameless classmate's obsession had taken a tangible form, and the boundary between admiration and intrusion blurred into a disconcerting silhouette.

She sought solace in the familiar confines of Mr. Sterling's office, where their forbidden connection unfolded against the backdrop of her rising literary success. As she shared the unsettling discovery, Mr. Sterling's eyes flickered with a mixture of concern and something darker—a spark of possessiveness.

"Selma," he murmured, his voice a low rumble, "this goes beyond admiration. It's an invasion of your privacy, a creation born from obsession. We need to tread carefully."

As the soap sculpture cast its voyeuristic gaze upon Selma, the news of her impending novel release heightened the anticipation. "Lightning in a Bottle" was poised to be a literary sensation, and she found herself preparing for a barrage of on-air interviews.

In the midst of interviews and promotional events, Selma's words became a dance of elegance, each sentence crafted to reveal just enough while concealing the depths of her forbidden connection with Mr. Sterling. The world awaited the revelation of her inspiration, unaware of the tempest that brewed beneath the polished facade.

Meanwhile, Mr. Sterling's obsession with the soap sculpture deepened. Its presence became a haunting reminder of the blurred lines between admiration and possessiveness. As Selma navigated the spotlight, the soap sculpture remained an unsettling specter, a symbol of the delicate dance they wove on the edge of forbidden desire.

In the weeks leading up to the novel's release, the soap sculpture incident hung in the air, an unresolved chord in the symphony of Selma's success. As the literary world prepared to be engulfed by the storm of "Lightning in a Bottle," the boundaries of their clandestine connection grew increasingly fragile, threatening to unravel with each passing moment.

Chapter Seven: Live Revelations

The air in the television studio hummed with excitement as Selma prepared for yet another on-air interview, a promotional endeavor for the upcoming release of "Lightning in a Bottle." The spotlight, bright and unforgiving, cast its gaze upon her as the interviewer, a charismatic co-host, steered the conversation toward fan engagement.

"And now, Selma, we have a surprise for you," the co-host announced with a twinkle in his eye, his grin hinting at a secret. "A gift from one of your dedicated fans."

A neatly wrapped package appeared on the table between them, its presence both intriguing and unsettling. Selma, accustomed to the unexpected in her recent journey to literary stardom, accepted the gift with a gracious smile.

As the paper unraveled, the studio audience held its breath in anticipation. The co-host's eyes twinkled with mischief as Selma uncovered another soap sculpture—a delicate and intricate rendition of her bust, captured in a moment of vulnerability.

The live audience erupted into a mix of gasps and giggles, their reactions mirroring the awkward tension that enveloped the studio. Selma, caught off guard, felt her cheeks flush with embarrassment. The co-host, oblivious to the discomfort, grinned and prompted her to share her thoughts.

"Well, this is certainly a unique gift," Selma quipped, her smile masking the unease beneath. "I guess my fans are getting quite creative in expressing their admiration. It's a testament to the power of inspiration, isn't it?"

The co-host chuckled, playing along with Selma's attempt to diffuse the situation. The live broadcast continued, but the soap sculpture incident lingered like a phantom, leaving Selma to grapple with the repercussions of her public unveiling.

Later that evening, after the bright lights of the studio had dimmed, Selma returned home, the echoes of the live broadcast still resonating in her mind. The soap sculpture, now an unexpected motif in her journey, found a place on her living room table, casting its silent gaze upon her.

Feeling a need to share her discomfort, she sought solace in the familiarity of Mr. Sterling's office. As she recounted the on-air revelation, his eyes betrayed a mix of concern and understanding.

"Selma," he said, his voice a soothing melody, "this goes beyond creativity. It's an invasion of your privacy, an unsettling echo of the soap sculpture incident at the academy. We can't let this continue."

She sighed, the weight of her public persona mingling with the complexities of their forbidden connection. "Mr. Sterling, it's like I'm trapped in a narrative where the lines between fiction and reality are blurred. How do I navigate this without losing myself?"

He leaned forward, his gaze a steady anchor. "Selma, your journey is a tempest, and sometimes, storms reveal the true nature of the landscape. We'll weather this together, but we must be cautious. The soap sculptures are a manifestation of something deeper, and we can't ignore the shadows they cast."

As Selma grappled with the soap-sculpted echoes of her newfound fame, the storm of her success continued to gather momentum, threatening to either catapult her to greater heights or consume her in the tumultuous waves of public scrutiny. In the dimly lit corners of Mr. Sterling's office, they faced the storm together, bound by a narrative that had become more intricate and perilous than either of them could have anticipated.

Chapter Eight: Unraveling Threads

The soap sculpture saga, once confined to the shadows, now emerged into the glaring spotlight of public scrutiny. Windhaven Academy, a bastion of privilege and prestige, found itself entangled in a web of scandal as images of the soap sculptures trended online, fueling speculation and gossip.

The school president, a figure with a reputation to uphold, reached out to Mr. Sterling, the creative writing tutor whose guidance had unwittingly become a source of inspiration for the soap sculptures. In the hallowed halls of academia, where appearances held immense weight, the president sought answers.

"Mr. Sterling," the school president intoned with a furrowed brow, "we need to address this soap sculpture incident. It's becoming a matter of public concern, and we can't afford any more scandals tarnishing our reputation."

Mr. Sterling, calm and composed, assured the headmaster that he would handle the situation discreetly, promising to get to the bottom of the soap-sculpted mystery. Little did he know that this resolution would unravel the delicate threads of Selma's world even further.

Summoning the male student responsible for the soap sculptures, Mr. Sterling orchestrated a meeting with Selma, aiming to untangle the web of infatuation and obsession that threatened to cast a shadow over her literary success.

In the dimly lit office, Selma and the young student faced each other, the air heavy with anticipation. Mr. Sterling, the arbiter of their clandestine connection, presided over the uneasy encounter.

"Selma," the young student began, his voice trembling with a mix of nerves and desperation, "I created those sculptures as a gesture of admiration. I thought you'd appreciate the artistic expression of my feelings."

Selma, her patience waning, met his gaze with a fiery intensity. "Admiration doesn't justify invasion of privacy. Those sculptures crossed a line, and I won't tolerate being objectified in such a manner."

The young student, fueled by a tempest of unrequited emotions, erupted with a fiery temper. "You don't understand, Selma! I poured my heart into those sculptures. You'll regret not appreciating my feelings."

Mr. Sterling intervened, his tone a blend of authority and empathy. "This situation needs to be resolved with respect and understanding. Selma deserves to be treated with dignity, not as an object of obsession. Your feelings, while valid, cannot justify crossing boundaries."

As the heated encounter reached its zenith, Selma's resolve hardened. "I cannot reciprocate feelings that I do not share. I value your creativity, but this infatuation has to end."

The young student, a storm of emotions raging within him, left the office with a parting shot. "You'll regret this, Selma. You'll see."

Left in the wake of the confrontation, Selma and Mr. Sterling faced the aftermath of unraveling threads. The soap sculptures, born from infatuation and admiration, had cast a shadow over the delicate dance they had woven in the hidden corners of Windhaven Academy. As the storm of scandal continued to swirl, the consequences of their forbidden connection became increasingly unpredictable, threatening to alter the course of their narratives in unforeseen ways.

Chapter Nine: Moonlit Tryst

Amid the tempest of public scrutiny and private tumult, Selma sought refuge in the quiet haven of a moonlit night. A secret tryst beckoned, a rendezvous with Mr. Sterling at the edge of a secluded pond, embraced by the serenade of willows and the silver glow of the moon.

The dock, a wooden stage suspended over the water, creaked beneath their shared weight as they stood at the precipice of their clandestine desires. The moonlight danced on the ripples below, casting a silvery sheen that mirrored the secrets they harbored.

Their lips met in a passionate kiss, the echoes of their forbidden connection reverberating in the stillness of the night. The air, thick with anticipation, crackled with the electricity of unrestrained desire. Mr. Sterling's fingers traced the contours of Selma's skin, each touch a declaration of the tempestuous love that bound them.

Deciding to cast off the shackles of restraint, they shed their garments, the moonlight a witness to their daring escapade. In a synchronized dance, they descended into the cool embrace of the water, the midnight swim a baptism in the tempest of their love.

The pond, once a reflection of serenity, became the stage for their secret tryst—a tempestuous ballet of limbs entwined beneath the moonlit canopy. Selma's laughter, a melody that echoed through the willows, mingled with the splashes of water as they embraced the daring freedom of the moment.

Unbeknownst to them, the boy who had harbored misguided affections lurked in the shadows, hidden among the rustling willows. His eyes, filled with a mixture of envy and fascination, bore witness to the passion that unfolded before him.

As the night embraced their secret, Selma and Mr. Sterling, entwined in the tempest of their desires, stood on the edge of the pond, the moonlight reflecting the untamed beauty of their forbidden connection. The echoes of their clandestine tryst lingered, a haunting melody that would resonate through the corridors of Windhaven Academy, forever changing the narrative of their lives.

Chapter Ten: Carved Shadows

The corridors of Windhaven Academy echoed with an unsettling hush as Selma's literary triumph unfolded in the wake of her novel's release. "Lightning in a Bottle" soared off the shelves, a testament to the magnetic allure of her words. Praise and accolades rained upon her, but amidst the celebration, an ominous shadow loomed.

In the midst of Selma's success, the soap sculptures, once a bizarre fascination, took a disturbing turn. The boy, driven by an unsettling obsession, presented Mr. Sterling with a creation that transcended the boundaries of decency and veered into the realm of the macabre.

A package arrived at Mr. Sterling's doorstep, the contents a grotesque manifestation of the boy's delusional mind. As he unwrapped it, a full-body soap sculpture of himself stood revealed—a detailed carving depicting him in a state of undress, standing on the edge of a dock. The unnerving precision hinted at a level of obsession that transcended mere infatuation.

Selma, standing by Mr. Sterling's side as the grotesque masterpiece was unveiled, felt a shiver crawl down her spine. The silent acknowledgment between them spoke volumes—the boy's actions had transcended the realm of misguided affection, revealing a disturbing depth of sociopathy.

"This is beyond anything we've dealt with before," Mr. Sterling muttered, his gaze locked on the soap sculpture. "We need to involve the authorities. This goes beyond the boundaries of school discipline."

As they grappled with the unsettling reality, Selma, stoic in the face of public praise, found herself unraveling in private. The soap sculptures, now an insidious manifestation of a disturbed mind, cast a dark shadow over her success. The lines between reality and the fiction she had penned blurred, and the tempest of her emotions threatened to consume her.

She retreated to Mr. Sterling's office, seeking solace in the sanctuary they had crafted amidst the storm. "Mr. Sterling, this is getting out of control. How do we protect ourselves from this madness?"

His eyes, reflecting a mixture of concern and determination, met hers. "Selma, we'll take every necessary step to ensure our safety. This is not just an infatuation; it's a dangerous obsession that requires swift and decisive action."

As the soap sculpture incident unfolded, the narrative of Selma's success and the shadows of her private turmoil danced in discordant harmony. The echoes of her novel, hailed as a literary triumph, mingled with the disquieting whispers of a sociopath's obsession.

In the corridors of Windhaven Academy, where privilege and ambition mingled with the untamed spirit of rebellion, Selma and Mr. Sterling faced a foe that transcended the boundaries of reason. The soap sculptures, grotesque manifestations of a disturbed mind, cast a chilling spell over their clandestine connection, threatening to unravel the very fabric of their forbidden love.

Chapter Eleven: Shadows Confronted

The air hung heavy with tension as Mr. Sterling, resolute in the face of the escalating soap sculpture saga, confronted the boy in a private meeting. In the dimly lit corners of Windhaven Academy, the two figures faced each other, man to man, the weight of unspoken turmoil lingering between them.

"Enough is enough," Mr. Sterling asserted, his voice cutting through the stillness. "These soap sculptures have crossed a line, and I won't tolerate this any longer. If it happens again, I'll involve the authorities. Do you understand?"

The boy, a cipher of obsession and resentment, met Mr. Sterling's gaze with a defiant glint in his eyes. "You can't stop what's already in motion, Mr. Sterling. Your secrets, Selma's secrets—they're not as hidden as you think."

A cold realization settled over Mr. Sterling. "What are you talking about? This ends here and now."

The boy leaned in, his voice a venomous whisper. "I may not have recorded your little rendezvous at the pond, but I saw everything. If you don't want the world to know about your forbidden affair, I suggest you tread carefully."

Mr. Sterling's jaw clenched with anger; his patience tested to its limits. "You're playing with fire, and you have no idea of the consequences. This is the final warning. If you take this any further, the police will be involved."

As the two men parted ways, the ominous threat hung in the air like a storm brewing on the horizon. Mr. Sterling, burdened with the weight of their clandestine connection, faced a foe who wielded the shadows as both weapon and shield.

In the dimly lit confines of his office, Mr. Sterling grappled with the ramifications of the boy's threat. The soap sculptures, once a bizarre manifestation of infatuation, had evolved into a weaponized narrative that threatened to unravel the delicate fabric of his and Selma's clandestine connection.

As the echoes of their forbidden tryst and the soap sculpture saga reverberated through Windhaven Academy, the shadows deepened, casting a veil over the untamed tempest of their illicit affair. The storm, both external and internal, gathered momentum, promising either revelation or destruction in its wake.

Chapter Twelve: Shadows on Display

In the dimly lit corners of Mr. Sterling's office, a beautiful and eerie display emerged—a shelf adorned with the soap sculptures that had once cast shadows of obsession and turmoil over their lives. The grotesque carvings, transformed into macabre art, now stood as silent witnesses to the tempestuous narrative that unfolded within Windhaven Academy.

Driven by an insatiable desire to reclaim the narrative, Mr. Sterling immersed himself in the creation of a novel that danced on the edge of the macabre. Romance, obsession, and infatuation intertwined in the narrative, with the soap sculptures at its heart, immortalized as haunting symbols of clandestine desires.

As he poured his soul into the manuscript, Mr. Sterling felt the weight of his own forbidden connection reflected in the words. The story, a mirror of their lives, blurred the lines between fiction and reality, pushing the boundaries of societal norms and unleashing a tempest that both intrigued and unsettled.

The novel, a masterpiece that transcended the boundaries of conventional storytelling, rested on the precipice of something great. Yet, as the words flowed from his pen, Mr. Sterling grappled with the moral dilemma of sharing the creation with Selma, knowing that it would force her to relive the shadows of their illicit affair.

Unable to find the words to reveal his literary endeavor, Mr. Sterling kept the novel a secret from Selma, the weight of his silence echoing through the hollowed halls of Windhaven Academy. The soap sculptures, now both symbols of artistic expression and the macabre reality of their lives, stood as sentinels on the shelf, silent witnesses to the drama that unfolded within the school's walls.

As the manuscript neared completion, Mr. Sterling hesitated before submitting it to a publisher. The fear of exposing their forbidden connection gnawed at him, but the allure of literary recognition proved irresistible. The novel, with its blend of romance and shadows, was sent into the world, a creation that promised to captivate and disturb.

To his surprise, the publisher not only embraced the story but hailed it as a work of genius. The novel, titled "Shadows on Display," was set to become Mr. Sterling's ticket to literary fame. The shadows that had haunted Windhaven Academy now took on a life of their own, immortalized in the pages of his creation.

As the news of the book deal spread, Mr. Sterling grappled with the inevitability of Selma discovering the narrative that laid bare their forbidden connection. The shadows, once confined to the soap sculptures, now stretched across the literary landscape, casting a dark and undeniable truth that threatened to engulf them both in a tempest of revelation and consequence.

Chapter Thirteen: Sculpting Shadows

The air in Mr. Sterling's office shimmered with anticipation as he presented the publishing contract to Selma, the gateway to literary recognition and fame. A radiant smile adorned her face as she scanned the document, excitement bubbling within her.

"I knew it was just a matter of time," she exclaimed, her eyes sparkling with delight. "Our story is so captivating, and now the world will know it too!"

As Selma's excitement reached its peak, she turned to Mr. Sterling with an eager glint in her eyes. "Can I read the manuscript? I can't wait to see how you've captured our story."

A weight settled in Mr. Sterling's chest as he hesitated, grappling with the impending revelation. "Selma, there's something I need to tell you before you read it. The novel, 'Shadows on Display,' is inspired by our story. It delves into the shadows of our forbidden connection, blurring the lines between reality and fiction."

Selma's enthusiasm waned, replaced by a furrowed brow. "What do you mean, inspired by our story? Is it not our story?"

Mr. Sterling took a deep breath, his eyes locking with hers. "It draws from our experiences, our connection, but it's not an exact replica. I took creative liberties to explore the nuances and emotions within the narrative."

A wave of anger swept over Selma's face; her disappointment palpable. "You wrote our story without telling me? How could you, Mr. Sterling?"

He held up his hands, a gesture of both apology and defense. "I wanted to reclaim the narrative, Selma. The soap sculptures, the rumors—our story was being told in dubious ways. I thought this novel would give us a chance to control our own narrative."

Selma's anger simmered, but a flicker of understanding danced in her eyes. "You could have told me, Mr. Sterling. We could have made this decision together."

As they grappled with the revelation, a sudden intrusion disrupted the fragile peace. A package, containing yet another soap sculpture, arrived with ominous implications. Selma and Mr. Sterling exchanged wary glances as they unwrapped the grotesque creation—a sculpture depicting the two of them entangled in a passionate embrace, legs and arms intertwined, and Mr. Sterling fully erect.

A gasp escaped Selma's lips, her face contorting with a mix of shock and revulsion. "This has gone too far, Mr. Sterling. We can't escape these shadows, no matter how hard we try."

The room, once filled with the promise of literary success, now echoed with the haunting presence of a distorted reflection of their forbidden connection. The soap sculptures, immortalizing their love in a macabre form, cast shadows that threatened to consume the delicate balance they had sought to.

Chapter Fourteen: Unveiling Shadows

In the aftermath of the revelation, Selma and Mr. Sterling stood at the precipice of a new chapter in their lives. The truth laid bare, their clandestine affair confessed, Mr. Sterling faced the consequences of his actions. The academy's administration, recognizing the delicate nature of their narrative, chose to sever ties with him.

The decision to move in together became an inevitable step in reclaiming control over the narrative they had once concealed. As they settled into a shared space, the shadows of secrecy lifted, and a newfound sense of freedom emerged. Together, they faced the daunting reality of a world eager to dissect the intricacies of their forbidden connection.

A book tour loomed on the horizon, a journey that would thrust them into the public eye. Embracing the irony, they decided to showcase the soap sculptures—the very symbols of their tumultuous love—as part of the narrative they sought to control. The world, curious and captivated, clamored for a glimpse of the art that had transcended obsession and desire.

To their surprise, the soap sculptures were met with both shock and awe. The art community, recognizing the intricate craftsmanship and the unique story they told, celebrated the sculptures as a bizarre yet undeniable form of artistic expression. As whispers of their unconventional exhibit spread, a prominent art museum in New York City extended an invitation to display the soap sculptures—an opportunity that could catapult their story to new heights.

Embracing the unexpected turn of events, Selma and Mr. Sterling agreed to the museum's proposal. The soap sculptures, once shrouded in shadows, were now destined to be showcased in the grandeur of a renowned art institution.

As the preparations for the exhibit unfolded, a storm brewed on the fringes of their lives. The mentally disturbed boy, consumed by the shadows of obsession and rejection, reached a boiling point. In a desperate bid for attention and revenge, he brought a knife to school, a final act of defiance that shattered the fragile balance they had fought so hard to maintain.

The academy, recognizing the severity of the situation, expelled the troubled boy, severing the last lingering ties to their tumultuous past. As the soap sculptures found their place in the hallowed halls of the New York City art museum, Selma and Mr. Sterling faced the consequences of their choices—a narrative rewritten, shadows unveiled, and a love that defied societal norms.

The book tour, now a journey of redemption and revelation, awaited them. The world, captivated by the soap sculptures and the scandalous love story they embodied, watched with bated breath as Selma and Mr. Sterling stepped into the spotlight, no longer confined by the shadows that once threatened to consume them.

Chapter Fifteen: Shadows Dissolved

In the wake of the expelled boy's desperate act, the tranquility of the academy shattered like glass. Drifting in the river, his lifeless body became a silent testament to the shadows that had consumed him. The water, a reflective canvas, cradled the boy's form in its arms, while the world above seemed oblivious to the tragedy that had unfolded.

The discovery of the boy's body cast a somber tone over the academy, the echoes of his tortured existence reverberating through the corridors. Alone, a tragic figure had met his end, his silent scream lost in the gentle current that carried him away.

As the autopsy unfolded, the revelation was as macabre as it was poetic. Eight intricately carved soap sculptures, hidden within the boy's stomach, told a tale of obsession that had transcended reason. The lye soap, a symbol of the very art that had consumed him, had eaten away at his insides, a creative and morbid culmination of his twisted desires.

In the hallowed halls of the New York City art museum, the soap sculptures that had once caused turmoil found a new home, showcased in the grandeur of artistic appreciation. The world, captivated by the haunting beauty of the soap sculptures, marveled at the twisted narrative they wove—a tragic story etched in lye and desire.

Meanwhile, on the cusp of literary fame, Selma and Mr. Sterling stood hand in hand at a sold-out book signing event. The scent of freshly printed pages and the murmur of an eager crowd surrounded them. With each signature, they forged a new chapter, leaving the shadows of their past behind.

"Who would have thought our story would lead us here?" Selma mused, her eyes meeting Mr.

Sterling's with a mixture of gratitude and resilience.

He smiled, a subtle acknowledgment of the tumultuous journey they had navigated together. "Creativity, Selma, it's a tempestuous force. It can carve shadows, but it can also illuminate the path forward."

As they signed books, the pen strokes became a dance of redemption, a celebration of their narrative reborn. The world, once captivated by scandal and shadows, now embraced the love story that had defied societal norms.

The final chapter unfolded with the closing of the book, leaving the echoes of a tale that had stretched the boundaries of love and art. Selma and Mr. Sterling, bound by a connection forged in secrecy and revealed in the light, stepped into the embrace of their newfound success.

The world watched as the story faded, the shadows dissolved, and the characters, once entangled in a tempest of desire, found solace in the gentle rhythm of their shared narrative. In the quiet moments between pages, the echoes of their journey lingered, a testament to the enduring power of a love that had weathered the storms and emerged, triumphant, into the warmth of a new

beginning.

Awake At a Wake

A Short Story

By Cal Sherwood

Chapter One: Fool's Errand

The day had started like any other for Jake Stanton, a man whose life had been defined by an unfortunate combination of recklessness and bad luck. As the sun dipped below the horizon, casting an amber glow across the city, Jake found himself entangled in a foolish escapade that would ultimately lead to his untimely demise.

In the heart of the city, a dilapidated warehouse stood like a forgotten relic of a bygone era. Its crumbling walls whispered stories of clandestine dealings and forgotten secrets. It was here, in the dimly lit alley adjacent to the warehouse, that Jake's ill-fated adventure began.

A misplaced sense of curiosity and a dash of liquid courage had propelled Jake into the clandestine world of a local gang's turf. Unbeknownst to him, the warehouse harbored a secret meeting of rival factions engaged in a bitter dispute over territory and illicit trades. The air was thick with tension as Jake, fueled by a cocktail of bravado and naivety, tiptoed through the shadows, convinced that he was on the verge of discovering something extraordinary.

Dressed in dark clothing that seemed out of place against the urban backdrop, Jake slinked along the edges of the warehouse, his heart pounding in sync with the distant beats of the city. The flickering glow of neon lights painted a surreal scene as he ventured deeper into the unknown.

Little did Jake know, his presence had not gone unnoticed. Unseen eyes tracked his every move, and whispers of suspicion echoed through the hidden corridors of the criminal underworld. The warehouse, once a silent witness to countless secrets, now held its breath, anticipating an inevitable collision between the unsuspecting intruder and the dangerous forces converging within.

As Jake reached the heart of the warehouse, the air grew heavy with the acrid scent of tension. He stumbled upon the clandestine gathering, a tableau of darkened silhouettes engaged in a heated exchange of hushed voices and guarded glances. Oblivious to the peril he had stumbled upon, Jake marveled at the unfolding drama before him, his eyes wide with a mixture of awe and foolish delight.

In a misguided attempt to prove his audacity, Jake decided to document the scene with his smartphone. The faint glow of the screen illuminated his face, casting shadows that danced with the uncertainty of the situation. Unbeknownst to him, a pair of menacing eyes locked onto his every move, a silent predator sizing up its prey.

It was then that the illusion shattered, and the warehouse erupted into chaos. Jake, realizing the gravity of his situation, attempted to retreat, but it was too late. The hostile whispers turned into enraged shouts, and the once-hidden figures emerged from the shadows, their intentions clear and menacing.

In the ensuing pandemonium, a single gunshot rang out, tearing through the night like a thunderclap. The air hung heavy with the acrid scent of gunpowder as Jake crumpled to the ground, a victim of his own ill-conceived adventure. The gang dispute, momentarily forgotten, now pivoted to a new focal point—the lifeless body of the unwitting intruder.

As Jake's vision blurred and the world around him faded to black, the realization of his own folly dawned upon him. In the final moments of his life, he pondered the senselessness of the journey that had led him to this grim fate—a fool's errand that had cost him everything.

Chapter Two: A Funeral's Revelation

The dimly lit room resonated with hushed conversations and sorrowful sighs as mourners gathered to bid farewell to Jake Stanton. The air was heavy with grief, a palpable weight that seemed to seep into the very fabric of the funeral home. The casket, adorned with flowers, stood as a silent testament to a life cut short by the foolish pursuit of curiosity.

Amidst the subdued atmosphere, Jake found himself drawn to the front of the room, standing beside his own lifeless body. A surreal sense of detachment enveloped him as he observed the tear-streaked faces and somber expressions of the mourners. At that moment, an otherworldly presence manifested itself—the Devil, resplendent in Mardi Gras colors, and a figure bathed in divine light—the embodiment of God.

"Jake Stanton," the Devil sneered with a mischievous glint in his eye. "You've got a front-row seat at your own funeral. What a show, huh?"

God, radiating an aura of compassion, stepped forward. "Jake, you've found yourself in a peculiar situation. You were murdered, and in the face of injustice, we offer you a chance at redemption."

The gravity of the situation began to sink in as God and the Devil explained that Jake had the opportunity to confess 30 sins, each one reflecting on the people present at his funeral. A chance to cleanse his soul and avoid the clutches of hell.

"You start with the sins, and as you confess, those affected will forgive you, placing a flower in your coffin," God explained, his voice resonating with kindness.

Jake nodded, his curiosity now replaced with a newfound sense of responsibility. The Devil cracked a wicked grin, eager to witness the unfolding drama.

With a deep breath, Jake began his confession. "I, uh, I once refused to let a guy leave work early. He used to work for me, and his grandmother was in the hospital. I denied him the chance to say goodbye, and she passed away while he was stuck at work."

A ripple of shock passed through the room as the mourners exchanged glances, unknowingly connected to Jake's revelation. A man in the audience, visibly moved, stood up, placed a white lily in the coffin, and whispered, "I forgive you."

The weight on Jake's shoulders lightened, but a profound sorrow lingered in the room. God nodded approvingly, acknowledging the first step towards redemption.

"Now, Jake, there's another sin," the Devil prodded, relishing in the unfolding drama. "Spill the beans, and let's keep this confessional rolling."

Jake hesitated, grappling with the guilt of another transgression. "I, uh, I once spread a rumor about a co-worker, tarnishing her reputation. It was petty, and I did it out of spite."

As the words left his lips, a woman in the crowd stood up, placed a single rose in the coffin, and uttered, "I forgive you."

The room held its collective breath, the air pulsating with a strange mix of sorrow and absolution. God and the Devil observed, one with compassion and the other with a twisted sense of satisfaction. The journey to redemption had only just begun, and Jake felt the weight of his past sins lifting, one confession at a time. The Devil, though amused, knew that the real challenges lay ahead, waiting to be unveiled in the chapters of Jake's confessional journey.

Chapter Three: Shadows of the Soul

The air in the funeral home hung with a tension both palpable and ominous. As Jake continued his confessional journey, the weight of his sins lifted gradually, like the shroud of darkness being peeled away layer by layer. God and the Devil observed, each with their own vested interest in the unfolding drama.

God, bathed in radiant light, spoke with an air of compassion. "Jake, the path to redemption is paved with honesty and remorse. Confess your sins, and let the healing begin."

The Devil, dressed in Mardi Gras colors, leaned forward, his eyes dancing with malevolence. "Oh, this is getting interesting. Let's see what other skeletons you've got in that closet of yours."

Jake, aware that the revelations were far from over, squared his shoulders and faced the assembly of mourners. "I... I once embezzled money from the company I worked for," he admitted, glancing around the room to gauge the reactions.

A murmur of surprise swept through the attendees, and a former business partner of Jake's, a man named Richard, stood up. He placed a carnation in the coffin, his gaze steady. "I forgive you," Richard declared, his forgiveness echoing in the cavernous space.

The weight on Jake's conscience lifted, but the Devil's eyes gleamed with anticipation. "Go on, Jake. Don't keep us waiting."

The confessions deepened as Jake delved into the shadows of his soul.

"I manipulated a friend into taking the blame for something I did in college," Jake confessed, his voice carrying the weight of remorse. A college buddy, now standing in the audience, placed a daisy in the coffin and said, "I forgive you."

The Devil chuckled, relishing in the revelation of these intricate webs of deceit. God, on the other hand, offered a reassuring nod, acknowledging the progress Jake was making.

As Jake continued his confessions, the sins became more sinister, the shadows darker.

"I cheated on my wife," he admitted, casting his eyes down in shame. The room tensed, and his wife, sitting in the front row, looked up with tearful eyes. She placed a single tulip in the coffin and whispered, "I forgive you."

The Devil, with a sly grin, commented, "Ah, the classic infidelity. How original."

Jake pressed on, steeling himself for the darker revelations that lay ahead. "I... I sabotaged a colleague's career to advance my own. I spread false rumors, manipulated situations. It ruined his life," he confessed, his voice faltering.

The colleague in question, now a broken man standing amidst the crowd, placed a violet in the coffin and uttered, "I forgive you."

The Devil, growing impatient, prodded Jake with a wry smile. "The clock is ticking, Jake. What else have you got?"

Sweat formed on Jake's forehead as he wrestled with the impending admission—the darker sin that lay at the core of his redemption. With a deep breath, he uttered the words he had long suppressed.

"I... I was involved in a hit-and-run accident. I fled the scene, leaving someone injured on the roadside," Jake confessed, his voice barely audible.

The room fell into a heavy silence, the gravity of Jake's revelation settling like a dense fog. A woman in the crowd, her face etched with sorrow, stood up. She placed a black rose in the coffin and, with a trembling voice, whispered, "I forgive you."

The Devil, sensing the crescendo of Jake's confessional journey, leaned in with a wicked grin. "Well, well, Jake. You're getting closer to the heart of darkness. What's next?"

Jake, beads of perspiration on his forehead, hesitated before uttering the words that carried the weight of a thousand sins. "I... I was indirectly responsible for a fire that claimed several lives. Negligence, greed, and shortcuts led to a building collapse, and people died."

The room gasped in collective horror, the atmosphere thickening with anguish. The Devil, for a moment, was taken aback by the gravity of Jake's admission. A man in the crowd, his face etched with grief, stood up, placed a blood-red rose in the coffin, and declared, "I forgive you."

As the weight lifted, a lingering darkness persisted. God's gaze held a mix of compassion and judgment. "Jake, your journey to redemption is not yet complete. Confess, and let the healing continue."

The Devil, despite the serious tone, couldn't resist a taunting comment. "What's next on the agenda, Jake? Murder? Betrayal? Speak up before I lose interest."

Jake, haunted by the depths of his transgressions, took a deep breath. "I... I caused the demise of a competitor's business by spreading false information and sabotaging their deals. It led to their bankruptcy and the ruin of their lives."

The competitor, a man who had lost everything, rose from his seat. With a heavy heart, he placed a wilted daffodil in the coffin and whispered, "I forgive you."

The confessional journey continued; each revelation more challenging than the last. A dark cloud seemed to dissipate with each forgiveness, yet an impending storm lingered on the horizon.

"I... I blackmailed a former employee to keep quiet about my shady dealings. I threatened to destroy their life if they spoke up," Jake confessed, the room recoiling at the revelation.

The former employee, now marked by the scars of Jake's manipulation, rose from the shadows. With a trembling hand, they placed a thistle in the coffin and uttered, "I forgive you."

The Devil, a shadowy figure reveling in the intricacies of human frailty, watched with amusement. "Time's ticking away, Jake. You're almost there."

As the confessions continued, the sins grew darker, more intricate, like a twisted tapestry unraveling to expose the darkest corners of Jake's soul. The Devil, ever eager for more, couldn't hide his delight.

"I...·I framed a family member for a crime they didn't commit. They served time in prison for my sins," Jake admitted, his voice breaking with remorse.

A family member, having borne the weight of Jake's deception, stood up. With tears in their eyes, they placed a forget-me-not in the coffin and whispered, "I forgive you."

The Devil, sensing the climax, grinned wickedly. "Jake, what's the grand finale? The pièce de résistance? The sin that will determine your fate?"

Jake hesitated, grappling with the darkest sin that loomed over him—the one that threatened to consume him entirely.

"I... I intentionally caused the death of a business rival by sabotaging their car," he confessed, his voice barely audible.

The room fell into a stunned silence, and the Devil's grin widened as if he had been waiting for this revelation all along. The rival's family, grief etched on their faces, rose from their seats. With a heavy heart, they placed a dark orchid in the coffin and whispered, "I forgive you."

The atmosphere, thick with the weight of the confessions, began to shift. The Devil, no longer the amused spectator, took a step forward.

"Jake Stanton, you've laid bare your sins, revealing the darkest corners of your soul. The question now is, can you face the ultimate truth?"

God, a beacon of compassion, looked at Jake with a gaze that held the promise of redemption. "Confess, Jake, and let the final revelation set you free."

Jake, standing on the precipice of damnation, took a deep breath. The Devil, with a sinister grin, awaited the revelation that would determine Jake's eternal fate.

"I... I killed a man. It was not an accident, not a moment of rage. I planned it, executed it, and watched him die," Jake confessed, the words hanging heavy in the air.

The room shuddered with the weight of the admission, and a man in the audience, connected to the revelation, stood up. He placed a pitch-black lily in the coffin and uttered, "I forgive you."

The Devil's grin faltered for a moment, replaced by a calculating stare. God, with unwavering compassion, nodded solemnly.

"You've confessed your sins, Jake," God declared. "The journey to redemption is not without its trials, but forgiveness has been granted. The path to salvation lies open to you."

As the weight of Jake's sins lifted, he felt a strange sense of release. The mourners, connected by the threads of forgiveness, watched as the shadows dissipated, leaving behind a man stripped bare of his darkest secrets.

The Devil, his composure regained, stepped forward. "Well, Jake, it seems you've earned a chance at redemption. But remember, redemption is not a one-time event. It's a continuous journey."

With a flick of his cane, the Devil vanished into the shadows, leaving Jake standing in the midst of forgiveness and absolution. God, a beacon of hope, spoke one final time.

"Jake Stanton, you are given a second chance. Use it wisely, for the path to redemption is a lifelong commitment. Seek forgiveness, mend the wounds you've caused, and may your soul find peace."

As the room began to fade, Jake felt a warm light enveloping him, carrying him away from the shadows of his past. The journey to redemption had just begun, and Jake, with the weight of his sins lifted, stepped into the uncertain embrace of a new chapter—one where forgiveness and redemption intertwined in the complex tapestry of his soul.

Chapter Four: The Poisoned Breakfast

As the first rays of dawn filtered through the curtains, Jake Stanton stirred from his sleep, his head throbbing with the aftermath of a night filled with questionable choices. The room seemed to spin for a moment, and as he blinked away the fog of his hangover, a surreal realization settled in—he had just experienced a vivid, life-altering dream.

Confused and disoriented, Jake propped himself up on his elbows, the fragments of the dream lingering in his mind like a fading mirage. He could almost hear the echoes of confessions, feel the weight of forgiveness, and sense the ominous presence of the Devil and the benevolence of God. It was as if the dream had been a cautionary tale, a surreal journey through the darkest recesses of his own conscience.

Shaking off the remnants of the dream, Jake swung his legs over the side of the bed and stumbled towards the bathroom. A cold splash of water on his face helped clear the lingering haze, but the dream still clung to the edges of his thoughts.

As Jake emerged from the bathroom, he found his wife, Lily, preparing breakfast in the kitchen.

The aroma of freshly brewed coffee and sizzling bacon filled the air, a stark contrast to the surreal dreamscape he had just left behind.

Lily looked up, her eyes sparkling with warmth. "Good morning, sleepyhead. Rough night?"

Jake managed a weak smile, still grappling with the strange blend of emotions stirred by the dream. "Yeah, something like that. I had the weirdest dream. It felt so real."

Seated at the breakfast table, Jake began to recount the dream to Lily, detailing the confessions, the forgiveness, and the ominous presence of the Devil and God. Lily listened attentively, her expression unwavering, masking the turmoil that brewed beneath the surface.

As Jake reached the point in the dream where he confessed to the affair, a heavy silence settled over the room. Lily's eyes, once warm and understanding, now glinted with a cold determination.

"And then, the big one, Lily," Jake hesitated, his voice catching in his throat. "I confessed to causing the death of a business rival."

Lily's gaze remained steady; her façade unbroken. "Go on, Jake. What happened next?"

"I felt a burning sensation in my throat," Jake continued, his voice growing faint. "It was like I was being punished for that sin. And then..." he trailed off, his eyes widening with realization.

The syrup bottle on the table, once innocent, now seemed to radiate a malevolent energy. Jake stared at it in horror as his throat began to convulse, the burning sensation intensifying.

"What's happening, Lily?" he choked out, panic coursing through him.

Lily, her eyes cold and resolute, watched with detached satisfaction as the poison took effect. "You see, Jake, dreams are just a reflection of our deepest fears and desires. In this case, a little dream gave me insight into your darkest secrets."

Jake clutched his throat, gasping for breath as the room spun around him. Lily stood up; her true intentions revealed.

"I found out about your affair, Jake," Lily admitted, her voice dripping with venom. "And in my dream, I discovered a way to make you pay for your sins."

As Jake's vision blurred and the edges of his consciousness faded, Lily leaned in, her voice a sinister whisper.

"I hope you enjoyed your dream, Jake, because reality is about to become a nightmare."

With those chilling words, Jake slumped forward, his world descending into darkness, the dream-turned-nightmare a twisted prelude to the vengeance his wife had exacted upon him.

Chapter Five: Welcome to Eternal Damnation

As Jake struggled for air, he realized with horror that the dream wasn't a mere figment of his imagination. It was a warning, a premonition of the impending doom. His vision blurred, the room spinning as he succumbed to the poison that now coursed through his veins.

As darkness closed in, he felt his body convulsing, his screams silenced by the unrelenting grip of death.

Suddenly, the shadows engulfed him, and Jake found himself in a realm of indescribable torment. The air reeked of sulfur, and eerie wails echoed through the abyss. The landscape, a desolate expanse of fiery pits, stretched as far as the eye could see. The flickering flames danced in macabre celebration, casting grotesque shadows on the jagged rocks.

Jake, disoriented and overwhelmed by the stench of burning brimstone, stumbled forward. A haunting figure emerged from the shadows—the Devil himself, waiting at the outer gates of Hell.

"Well, well, Jake Stanton. Fancy seeing you here," the Devil greeted with a smirk, his eyes gleaming with a perverse amusement.

"Where am I?" Jake demanded, his voice echoing in the infernal abyss.

The Devil chuckled, a sinister melody that reverberated through the damned landscape. "You're in Hell, my friend. The final destination for souls like yours."

"But... but I confessed! I sought redemption!" Jake protested, desperation in his voice.

The Devil raised an eyebrow, feigning surprise. "Oh, you did confess, indeed. But you see, Jake, the dream was a last-ditch effort from both God and me to give you a chance at redemption. You were meant to confess everything to Lily, the person you wronged the most."

Jake's mind reeled with the revelation. The dream, the confessions—it was all a test, and he had failed.

"You didn't make it to the last confession, Jake," the Devil continued, his tone mocking. "You were meant to confess to Lily about the hit-and-run, your final and darkest sin. But you choked on your own guilt before you could utter the words. A tragic end to your pitiful attempt at redemption."

As Jake absorbed the cruel truth, the Devil strolled beside him, the flames casting an eerie glow on his Mardi Gras-colored attire. "Now, Jake, welcome to your eternal damnation. Hell has a special place for those who squander their chances at redemption."

The landscape transformed as they walked, each step leading Jake deeper into the labyrinthine corridors of torment. He glimpsed lost souls writhing in agony, their anguished cries forming a cacophony that echoed through the cavernous depths.

"You see, Jake, Hell is not just fire and brimstone. It's the manifestation of your deepest fears, regrets, and sins," the Devil explained, his tone almost sympathetic. "Here, you'll experience the consequences of every wrongdoing, every pain you inflicted upon others."

As they delved deeper, Jake witnessed scenes from his own life, twisted and distorted into nightmarish spectacles. The man he had blackmailed, the family member he had framed, the lover he had betrayed—all tortured and tormented in grotesque displays of retribution.

The Devil, reveling in Jake's despair, spoke with a twisted glee. "Hell is a personalized experience, Jake. Every torment is tailor-made for the soul it embraces. Your sins have crafted a unique brand of eternal suffering just for you."

Jake, overwhelmed by the surreal horror unfolding before him, fell to his knees. "Is there no hope? No chance of redemption?"

The Devil chuckled, a sound devoid of compassion. "In Hell, redemption is but a distant fantasy. You had your chance, Jake, and you squandered it. Now, you're here to face the consequences of your choices."

As Jake sank into the depths of despair, the Devil leaned in, his voice a haunting whisper. "You'll be reliving your sins for eternity, Jake. No escape, no respite. Welcome to Hell."

Dukes Opus

By Cal Sherwood

Chapter 1: A Pup with a Purpose

The day I came into this world, destiny had a plan for me – a plan that would lead me through the harshest of trials and the warmest of embraces. I am Duke, a German Shepherd with a tale to tell, and today, on my last day on earth, I want to share the story of my life.

I was born with a heart full of hope and a spirit eager for adventure. At 1.5 years old, I found myself in the rigorous kennels of the Border Patrol program, a place where dreams of chasing bad guys collided with the harsh reality of training. Little did I know this would be the beginning of a journey that would shape me into the loyal companion I am today.

The kennels were a cacophony of barks, echoing off the cold, unforgiving walls. From the start, life was tough – a relentless routine of training, discipline, and correction. Shock collars became my constant companion, a painful reminder of the path I was meant to follow. The trainers were stern, their voices cold, their methods harsh.

Despite the adversity, I was determined to prove myself. I excelled in Drug, Bomb, and Cadaver School. My nose became my greatest asset, and I reveled in the praise and attention that followed each successful training session. But then came the takedown, the moment where I was expected to be fierce, unyielding. It was a test I couldn't pass, a challenge that revealed the essence of who I was – too friendly for the cold world of law enforcement.

The trainers saw my failure as a setback, a disappointment. To them, I was just another recruit unable to meet the standards set by their stringent program. But little did they know, it was my failure that led me to the greatest victory of my life.

One day, as I paced restlessly in my kennel, two figures walked in. Don and Charlie – a pair of kind eyes and open hearts. They were looking for a companion, a friend who would fill their lives with joy. I looked into their eyes, and they saw something in me that the Border Patrol trainers never did – a spirit yearning for love, a heart craving understanding.

And so, my life took a turn. Don and Charlie chose me, and in that moment, the cold walls of the kennel transformed into the warm embrace of a forever home. As I stepped into their world, the shock collars and beatings were replaced with gentle pats and soothing words. The love I had been denied for so long now enveloped me, mending the wounds of my past.

With Don and Charlie, I discovered the true purpose of my existence – not to be a fierce enforcer, but a loyal companion. Our bond grew stronger with each passing day, a testament to the healing power of love. The trials of the Border Patrol program became a distant memory, overshadowed by the warmth of a home filled with laughter, kindness, and unconditional acceptance.

As I reminisce about my life on this final day, I am grateful for the journey that brought me here. Don and Charlie gave me more than a home; they gave me a purpose and a family. Today may mark the end of my earthly adventures, but the love I found will forever echo in the hearts of those who shared this journey with me.

Chapter 2: The Trials of the Border Patrol Program

Life in the kennels was a harsh contrast to the warmth and love I now knew. The Border Patrol program was a place where discipline reigned supreme, and I, a failed recruit, was relegated to the sidelines. The concrete walls felt colder, the barks of my fellow inmates a constant reminder of the life I had left behind.

Each day began with rigorous training sessions, an unyielding routine that tested not only my physical prowess but also my mental resilience. The trainers were stern, demanding obedience without a hint of compassion. Shock collars became a part of my daily attire, delivering painful jolts whenever I strayed from their strict commands.

The takedown, the very act that had sealed my fate, haunted my every waking moment. I could still feel the weight of those failed attempts, the disappointed eyes of the trainers drilling into my soul. Yet, as I reflect on those times, I understand now that it was not a flaw but a testament to my true nature – a nature that would later find its purpose in a different kind of service.

Despite the brutality of the Border Patrol program, there were moments of triumph. I excelled in specialized training – Drug, Bomb, and Cadaver School. My keen senses and unwavering determination earned me the praise of the trainers. In those brief moments of success, I glimpsed a glimmer of hope, a belief that perhaps there was a place for me in the world of service.

Yet, the respite was short-lived. The trainers, fixated on the failed takedown, dismissed my achievements. To them, I was an anomaly, a deviation from their rigid expectations. As the days turned into weeks and weeks into months, I felt the weight of their disappointment bearing down on me.

The kennels were not just a physical confinement; they were a cage for my spirit. However, fate had other plans for me. It was a day like any other when Don and Charlie walked into my life. Their eyes met mine, and in that moment, they saw beyond the scars of the Border Patrol program. They saw a survivor, a spirit yearning for liberation from the chains of harsh discipline.

Don and Charlie chose me, and with their decision, the heavy doors of the kennels creaked open to a world of kindness and acceptance. As I left that dark chapter behind, I embraced the warmth of their home, where shock collars were replaced by gentle touches and beatings substituted with affectionate pats.

In the embrace of my new family, I learned that life was not about harsh discipline but about understanding, compassion, and the unspoken language of love. The trials of the Border Patrol program had toughened my exterior, but it was the kindness of Don and Charlie that mended the wounds within.

As I settled into my forever home, I realized that my journey was far from over. The trials had sculpted me, but it was the love that defined me. In their company, I found a purpose beyond the expectations of the Border

Patrol program – a purpose that would leave an indelible mark on the hearts of those who welcomed me into their lives.

Chapter 3: Finding Home

Fort Knox, Kentucky, became the backdrop of the next chapter in my life. Don and Charlie, along with their loyal companion, me, found ourselves stationed in a place that would become synonymous with happiness, freedom, and unconditional love. The ranch-style house they chose as our home was surrounded by sprawling fields, and a tranquil pond mirrored the peace that now enveloped our lives.

The house was a sanctuary, a stark contrast to the rigid walls of the Border Patrol kennels. Here, there were no shock collars or stern trainers, only the freedom to run, play, and bask in the sunlight. The absence of fences allowed me to roam without restraint, the wind carrying the scent of freedom that filled my nostrils.

As we settled into our new home, I discovered the joy of simple pleasures – the feeling of grass beneath my paws, the coolness of the pond's water, and the warmth of the sun on my fur. Life at Fort Knox was a far cry from the harshness of the Border Patrol program, and I reveled in every moment of it.

The house, with its inviting ranch-style design, became the backdrop for countless memories.

It was a place of laughter, shared meals, and the comforting embrace of my two dads. But amidst the newfound freedom and happiness, a peculiar habit emerged.

I formed an unbreakable bond with Charlie, and as much as I loved both Don and Charlie, there was an inexplicable attachment to the latter. It was as if Charlie held the key to my heart, and I couldn't bear to be separated from him, even for a moment.

Whenever Charlie decided to leave the house, a sense of restlessness would overcome me. The garage door became the barrier between me and the person I loved most in the world.

Determined to be near Charlie, I devised a plan – a plan that involved breaking into the garage.

It started innocently enough, a few scratched doors and some damaged doorframes, but my determination knew no bounds. Don and Charlie soon found themselves facing a series of renovations, with doors and frames bearing the scars of my quest to be close to Charlie.

After a few rounds of repairs, the two dads realized the depth of my attachment and the extent of my intelligence. It became a routine – whenever Charlie left, I would find my way into the garage, eagerly awaiting his return. It was a gesture of love, a way of saying, "I missed you, and I'm here to welcome you home."

As the garage doors and frames accumulated their battle scars, Don and Charlie came to a realization – locking the doors was futile. They learned to appreciate my intelligence, understanding that my love for Charlie was a force that couldn't be contained by mere locks and barriers.

And so, the garage became my waiting room, a place where anticipation met unconditional love. Every time they returned, whether it was from a day's work or a brief errand, they would find me there – tail wagging, eyes sparkling, ready to shower them with the boundless affection that filled my canine heart.

In the rhythm of our everyday lives at Fort Knox, the garage became a symbol of the unbreakable bond we shared. It wasn't just about waiting; it was about the joy of reunion, a moment that echoed the profound connection between a loyal dog and the family that had given him a second chance at happiness.

Chapter Four: Three Days of Solitude

The day Charlie left for a business trip to Las Vegas marked a shift in the atmosphere at home. As he packed his bags, Duke's eyes reflected a subtle sadness, an unspoken understanding that his beloved companion would be absent for a while. For three days, it would be just Don and Duke, navigating the familiar spaces without Charlie's lively presence.

As the days unfolded, Duke's usual enthusiasm waned. His tail, once a joyful flag of his spirit, now hung low. He roamed the house, a touch of melancholy in his every step. The absence of

Charlie's comforting energy left a void that even Duke's playful antics couldn't entirely fill.

In the evenings, Duke developed a peculiar routine. Instead of joining Don in the living room, he sought refuge in the master closet. There, among Charlie's clothes, he curled up in a ball, finding solace in the scent that lingered on the fabric. It became his haven, a quiet place where he could feel close to the one who was temporarily absent.

Don observed Duke's subdued behavior, his heart growing heavy with each passing day. When Charlie finally returned, Don shared the tale of Duke's three days of solitude. The revelation struck a chord, and they realized just how deeply Duke felt the absence of Charlie.

During Charlie's trip, Duke exhibited a loyalty that surpassed the boundaries of routine. Each night, he slept on Charlie's side of the bed, as if keeping a silent vigil for his return. In the daytime, he stationed himself by the window, gaze fixed on the driveway, awaiting the moment Charlie would walk through the door.

The realization dawned upon Don and Charlie that Duke's loyalty was not just a display of attachment but a profound connection that mirrored the strength of their family bonds. Duke, in his own silent way, had weathered the days of solitude, a testament to his unwavering devotion.

As Charlie embraced Duke, it was evident that the bond between them had deepened. Duke's actions spoke louder than any words could convey, revealing a level of loyalty and love that enriched their understanding of the four-legged member of their family. In those three days of solitude, Duke had taught them a valuable lesson about the depth of companionship and the resilience of love.

Chapter Five: Thanksgiving Bonds

The road to Lebanon, Virginia, stretched before us, winding through landscapes adorned with the hues of autumn. Don, Charlie, and I embarked on a Thanksgiving road trip to join Don's family for a feast that would not only fill our stomachs but also our hearts.

As we reached our destination, a cozy home filled with the warmth of family traditions, I sensed the anticipation in the air. Don's family welcomed us with open arms, and the aroma of a Thanksgiving feast wafted through the air, promising a celebration of gratitude and togetherness.

Amidst the laughter and joy, I couldn't help but notice the presence of Don's mother, Brenda. She radiated a certain gentleness, her eyes reflecting a lifetime of stories and experiences. Little did I know that this Thanksgiving would mark the beginning of a beautiful bond between us.

As the family gathered around the table, the atmosphere was charged with the spirit of gratitude. I, too, took my place among them, my tail wagging in sync with the festive mood. However, my attention soon gravitated toward Brenda. There was a certain vulnerability in her eyes, a quiet longing for companionship that resonated with me.

Without hesitation, I approached Brenda, my senses attuned to her needs. It was as if an unspoken understanding passed between us. She extended her hand, and I nuzzled against it, a silent reassurance that in this moment, she wasn't alone. The room embraced a serene quietness as Brenda and I formed a connection that transcended words.

Throughout the Thanksgiving celebration, Brenda and I became inseparable. I followed her like a shadow, my presence a source of comfort. Whether it was a gentle pat on my head or a shared moment of stillness, our bond grew stronger with each passing hour.

Don and Charlie observed this connection with awe, realizing that I possessed a sensitivity that went beyond the ordinary. Brenda, in turn, found solace in my company, a companion who understood the language of silent companionship.

The significance of that Thanksgiving didn't go unnoticed. From that day forward, I became a constant presence during family gatherings, especially the holidays. My sensitivity to the needs of the elderly, particularly Brenda, had woven me into the fabric of the family traditions. I became a cherished member, offering not just companionship but a reminder of the enduring power of connection.

As we packed our bags to leave Lebanon, the echoes of laughter and the warmth of newfound bonds lingered. That Thanksgiving had not only filled our stomachs with delicious food but had also nourished our souls with the richness of connection and the enduring spirit of gratitude.

Chapter Six: A Noble Calling

Life in the tranquil haven of Fort Knox, Kentucky took an unexpected turn when I found my true calling. The Kentucky State Police recognized my unique talents, and I officially became a registered cadaver dog. Don and Charlie, already proud pet parents, found a new sense of pride in my newfound purpose.

As the Kentucky State Police began to call on my services, our home transformed into a hub of activity. The house that once echoed with the laughter of two now resonated with the presence of three working men, each contributing to the welfare of our little family.

My training kicked into high gear as I accompanied the police on missions to locate missing persons or recover those who had met untimely fates. The scent of my fellow humans became a puzzle to solve, a challenge I embraced with the dedication of a loyal companion. The weight of responsibility settled on my shoulders, and I approached each mission with a seriousness that mirrored the gravity of my task.

Don and Charlie, my unwavering supporters, beamed with pride at my achievements. They marveled at the transformation of a failed recruit into a valuable asset for the community. Our home became a hub of celebration whenever news of a successful mission reached us. In the eyes of my humans, I wasn't just a pet; I was a hero, making a difference in the lives of those in need.

The neighborhood, too, became familiar with the sight of me donning my working gear, ready to assist the Kentucky State Police in their endeavors. Residents would nod in acknowledgment, knowing that the diligent German Shepherd from down the street was playing a crucial role in the safety of the community.

Despite the seriousness of my work, my connection with the community blossomed. Children would approach me with awe, and adults would express their gratitude for the service I provided. I had become more than just a pet; I was a symbol of hope, a living testament to the potential for redemption and purpose.

As the years passed, Don and Charlie continued to shower me with praise, fostering an environment of love and encouragement. Our home, once a refuge from the harsh realities of the world, had evolved into a haven for three hardworking souls bound by mutual respect and unwavering love.

My journey from the kennels of the Border Patrol program to the esteemed ranks of the Kentucky State Police cadaver dog was a testament to the resilience of the human-canine bond. In each mission, I found not just a sense of purpose but a deep connection with the world around me. And as I lay by the hearth after a day's work, I knew that the warmth of Don and Charlie's love was the greatest reward of all.

Chapter Seven: A Christmas Miracle

December arrived, casting a festive spell over the Blue Grass Parkway. It was a chilly day, and as Charlie drove along the winding road, he stumbled upon an unexpected sight—an 8-week-old Anatolian Shepherd puppy, alone and vulnerable in the middle of the asphalt.

Charlie's heart swelled with compassion as he pulled over, his concern growing for the tiny creature facing the cold world. He gently scooped her up, her small form fitting snugly in his arms. A mixture of emotions washed over him, and he knew he had to share this moment with Don.

Calling Don, tears welled in Charlie's eyes as he described the small, defenseless pup he had found. Don, sensing the urgency and the newfound love in Charlie's voice, simply said, "Bring her home."

And so, with a new passenger in tow, Charlie drove back, cradling the little pup against his chest. As he crossed the threshold of their home, the decision was made. They would keep her, and Don bestowed upon her the name "Angel."

Duke, initially skeptical of this new addition to the family, expressed his discontent with growls and bared teeth. The dynamics of the household shifted as Angel tentatively explored her new surroundings, her innocent eyes reflecting the uncertainty of her past.

But Duke's heart, as resilient as his spirit, softened over time. He recognized the vulnerability in Angel and, like a guardian angel himself, took her under his wing. Their bond evolved from initial skepticism to a beautiful friendship.

In the days that followed, Duke became Angel's mentor and protector. He taught her the ropes of their shared domain and, surprisingly, initiated her into the family's unique way of communication. Duke, with his wise demeanor, demonstrated how to alert Don and Charlie when nature called by tapping the door handle with a paw.

The transformation was remarkable. Angel, once a lonely pup on a desolate highway, became an integral part of the family, her spirit blending seamlessly with Duke's. Their playful antics echoed through the house, a harmonious melody of two souls finding companionship in unexpected places.

The family, now a trio, grew by one, and the love that enveloped their home expanded to embrace the newest member. As the winter winds whispered outside, Duke and Angel curled up together, their bond a testament to the transformative power of love and the magic that December brings. In the warmth of their shared moments, the family discovered that sometimes, the most precious gifts come in the form of unexpected miracles.

Chapter Eight: A Chapter of Surprises

Fort Leavenworth, Kansas, welcomed Don and Charlie with new orders and fresh opportunities. The four-level split-level house with a spacious backyard became their new home. Duke and Angel, already seasoned travelers, adapted to the change with their usual resilience.

As the seasons shifted and the routines of Command and General Staff College settled in, the household found a comfortable rhythm.

The spacious house echoed with laughter and the pitter-patter of four paws as Duke and Angel explored every nook and cranny of their new abode.

However, in the crisp October air, a surprise awaited. Angel, the bundle of joy who had entered their lives on the Blue Grass Parkway, went into heat. The unexpected twist in their plans set the stage for an eventful December 19th when Angel gave birth to a litter of five German Anatolian Shepherd puppies—two boys and three girls.

The arrival of the adorable pups should have been a cause for celebration, but it inadvertently became a strain on the dynamics of the household. Charlie and Don, navigating the challenges of new responsibilities and changes, found themselves facing the unexpected demands of a growing family.

Amidst the chaos, Duke emerged as a silent pillar of support. With his wise eyes and caring demeanor, he sensed the tension in the air. Whether it was a comforting nudge or a reassuring gaze, Duke offered solace to both Charlie and Don, acting as a mediator in the uncharted territories of parenthood.

The strains on Charlie and Don's relationship became evident, and the weight of the unforeseen circumstances pressed on them. Sleepless nights, puppy cries, and the added responsibilities of caring for a burgeoning family began to take a toll.

But Duke, the steadfast companion, was a source of comfort. His presence reminded them of the enduring strength of love, and his gentle gestures conveyed a message of understanding. In the midst of the challenges, Duke emerged as a beacon of stability, a reminder that no obstacle was insurmountable when faced with the unwavering support of family.

As the days unfolded, and the puppies grew into playful bundles of fur, the household slowly found its equilibrium. The strains on Charlie and Don's relationship began to ease, replaced by a shared understanding forged through adversity.

In Duke's watchful eyes, there was a silent promise – that love could weather storms, that challenges could be overcome, and that, in the end, the family would emerge stronger, their bonds tested and proven resilient. As the puppies tumbled and played, Duke stood as a testament to the enduring power of love in the face of unexpected surprises.

Chapter Nine: A Changing Skyline

The whirlwind of life continued as the puppies, each with their unique personalities, found their forever homes. Eris embarked on a new adventure with Jenny at the Pentagon, and Akira now lived in Indianapolis, under the care of Don's cousin Natasha. Louie, with his lively spirit, found a home with the director of the Veterinarian Clinic down the road. The house, once bustling with the pitter-patter of little paws, gradually settled into a quiet rhythm.

Charlie, the largest of them all, found a forever home with Tim and Palma, soon coming up on orders themselves for Fort Campbell, Kentucky.

As the puppies ventured into their new lives, Charlie and Don were left with Lucy, the little ball of fur who had become a permanent fixture in their hearts. Lucy, with her playful antics and affectionate nature, seamlessly blended into the ever-growing family, bringing a new dimension of joy and warmth to the household.

However, the military life held another surprise for the family. Orders arrived, directing them to Fort Meade, Maryland. The serene landscapes of Kansas would soon be exchanged for the bustling streets of Baltimore. A 4-level split-level and a spacious yard would give way to a beautiful 5-story, 4-bedroom, 4-bathroom brownstone across the street from Patterson Park.

The prospect of a new adventure stirred excitement in their hearts. Lucy, with her keen instincts, seemed to sense the change on the horizon. The family geared up for the move, bidding farewell to the familiar corners of their home and preparing to embrace the unknown.

The journey to Maryland marked a fresh chapter in their military life. Patterson Park, with its sprawling greenery and vibrant community, awaited them. The brownstone, a charming addition to the historical skyline of Baltimore, promised a new canvas for memories to unfold.

As boxes were packed and the house echoed with the laughter and chatter of farewells, Lucy watched with curious eyes. She had become an integral part of the family, witnessing the ebb and flow of their adventures. Little did she know, a new city awaited her playful paws and boundless energy.

With each step into the unknown, the family carried the lessons learned from their previous chapters. Love had been their constant companion, and as they approached the horizon of change, they did so with open hearts and the knowledge that, no matter where life led them, the bonds they had forged would remain unbreakable.

The brownstone in Baltimore awaited, a new canvas for the stories yet to unfold. And with Lucy by their side, the family ventured forward, ready to embrace the challenges and joys that awaited them in the charming cityscape of Fort Meade, Maryland.

Going Up

By Cal Sherwood

Chapter One: The Invisible Ascent

Chantry Chambers had always believed he was a mistake. Born into a world that seemed indifferent to his existence, he carried the weight of rejection, falsities, and empty promises on his young shoulders. His life unfolded as a series of unfortunate events, each one reinforcing the narrative that he was unwanted.

Every step he took seemed to echo the rattle of aspirin in his pocket, a symphony of despair. In his front left pocket, the bottle of aspirin served as a morbid companion, a constant reminder of the pain he sought to escape. In the front right pocket, a razor lay beneath athletic tape, a concealed instrument of self-inflicted release.

Chantry's intentions were clear as he ventured into the woods, a place where nature concealed both beauty and peril. The thorns of blackberry bushes tore at his skin, drawing blood that would soon mingle with the earth. His mind was set on a dark journey, driven by a desire to stain the world with his pain, torment, and indifference.

Yet, as he walked deeper into the forest, the surroundings took on an unexpected vibrancy. Crimson bled into the green leaves, blue berries, and the purple of wild lavender, creating a kaleidoscope of colors. It was as if the world itself was pushing back against the darkness within him.

His inner turmoil played out like a reel of haunting scenarios. Memories of a mother faced with an agonizing choice between her blue-eyed baby boy and heroin. The relentless voice in his head, more vicious than the external forces that pushed him to the brink.

As Chantry pushed through the thicket, a thorn caught his skin, opening a wound that bled with a color that seemed to symbolize the profound change within him. The forest, with its enchanting aroma, became a backdrop to his internal struggle.

His initial attempts to articulate his pain through writing resulted in 73 failed exoduses. The pen seemed to rebel against the act of documenting his despair. Frustration drove him to numb his senses with a joint laced with acid, opening the door to a surreal journey that would redefine his understanding of life and purpose.

Amidst the blackberry bushes, Chantry encountered a crow, a creature seemingly attuned to his inner turmoil. As he spoke to the bird, the forest took on a surreal quality, a place where reality and perception intertwined.

"You seem to get me... thank you," Chantry whispered to the crow, finding an unexpected solace in the presence of the enigmatic bird.

The crow, dismissive and disdainful, squawked and flew off into an opening, urging Chantry to follow. Each step weighed heavy, laden with the gravity of his intentions. The bottle of aspirin and razor in his pockets felt like anchors, pulling him toward the abyss he sought to escape.

As he approached the opening, the crow reappeared, its feathers shining in the sunlight. Chantry's path led to a discovery that defied logic—an intricate staircase in the heart of the forest. Gleaming brass railings and mahogany carvings adorned the mysterious structure, challenging the very fabric of reality.

"Hmmm...no support beams," Chantry mused, questioning the origin of this celestial staircase. The forest seemed to respond to his presence, its scents and colors intensifying. The surreal encounter with the crow and the emergence of the staircase fueled his sense of disorientation.

A decision loomed as Chantry, now high above the forest floor, contemplated the razor in his hand. The voice in his head, once relentless in its torment, now wavered in the face of an unexpected revelation. The forest, the staircase, and the cerulean sky above beckoned him to reconsider.

The world below watched as a man climbed invisible stairs, a spectacle that sparked chaos and curiosity. Mitch and his companion, tethered to a water tower, became unwitting witnesses to a phenomenon they struggled to comprehend.

The town, once a backdrop to Chantry's anguish, transformed into a stage for hysteria and wonder. Religious factions predicted the end of times, while the more populous cities grappled with their own chaos. But for Chantry, the ascent offered a new perspective, a journey from despair to self-discovery.

As he climbed higher, the chanting voices below became a chorus of humanity, yearning for connection. The invisible stairs became a beacon of hope, drawing people from near and far to witness the extraordinary. GOOOING UP!

GOOOOING UP! The chants echoed through the forest, unaware that the man they sought was on a descent.

For the first time, Chantry felt seen, not as a mistake or a stray, but as himself—Chantry Chambers. The weight that had anchored him to the ground now lifted, and he soared above the world that had once rejected him.

As he descended, the patches of mold below crystallized into people who had come to witness the spectacle. The bucolic cries on the wind were now voices of curiosity and awe. GOOOOING UP! The town, once indifferent to his existence, became a tapestry of faces looking up.

Chantry's life had taken a surreal turn, and the stairs that once symbolized escape now represented his second chance. The mirage of despair that haunted him faded as he descended, leaving behind a town forever changed by his ascent.

When he reached the bottom step, the sun began its descent, and the moon rose in the sky. From that summit, Chantry saw the world anew—a world where miracles happened in the most dubious of ways. The invisible stairs had served their purpose, leading him from the end to a new beginning.

As he stood on the last step, the razor blade in his hand lost its power. The once-compelling urge to end it all now seemed inconsequential. The end had become the beginning, and Chantry was ready to embrace the new chapter that awaited him.

The town, now in the grip of a newfound fascination, would never forget the man who climbed invisible stairs. Little did they know that Chantry Chambers, once a lost soul, had found his purpose in the most extraordinary ascent.

CHAPTER TWO: The Unseen Realm

Mitch and his companion, the witnesses from the water tower, watched as Chantry descended with a mix of confusion and awe. The world around him had changed, and the once-ordinary town now crackled with an energy that pulsed through the air.

The media, drawn by the spectacle, descended upon the town like a swarm of locusts. Journalists and cameramen jostled for the best angles, trying to capture the essence of the man who defied gravity. Religious leaders claimed divine intervention, and conspiracy theorists spun intricate webs of speculation.

Chantry, however, felt an unusual sense of detachment from the chaos that surrounded him. The weight of despair that once anchored him had lifted, replaced by a newfound purpose that he struggled to define. As the town's newfound curiosity swirled, Chantry retreated into the shadows, grappling with the impact of his extraordinary journey.

In the days that followed, Chantry found himself at the center of a media storm. Reporters hounded him for interviews, attempting to unravel the mystery behind the invisible staircase. News outlets speculated on the origin of this supernatural phenomenon, while psychologists debated the state of Chantry's mental health.

But amidst the fervor, Chantry remained silent. The cacophony of voices around him was a stark contrast to the quiet introspection he craved. He wandered through the town, feeling both a part of it and detached, as if he existed in a parallel reality.

A knock on his door one evening disrupted his solitude. Opening it, he found a middle-aged woman with a determined expression and a notepad in hand. She introduced herself as Lydia Turner, a reporter from a prominent news outlet.

"Chantry Chambers, the man who defied gravity. Mind if I ask you a few questions?" she inquired, already assuming permission by the way she held her notepad ready.

Chantry hesitated, glancing at the chaos outside his window before reluctantly inviting her in. Lydia entered, her eyes scanning the room for clues, for something that could explain the inexplicable.

As Lydia fired questions, Chantry found himself opening up in ways he hadn't anticipated. He shared fragments of his past, the pain that led him to the invisible staircase, and the transformative journey that followed. Lydia listened intently, her initial skepticism giving way to a genuine curiosity.

The story of Chantry Chambers, once a tale of despair, now unfolded as a narrative of resilience and self-discovery. The invisible staircase became a symbol not just of ascent but of rebirth. Lydia, sensing the depth of Chantry's experience, realized that the story transcended sensationalism—it held the potential to inspire.

As the night wore on, the two delved deeper into Chantry's past, unearthing memories long buried beneath layers of anguish. Lydia, typically objective and analytical, found herself captivated by the human behind the headline.

Days turned into weeks, and Chantry's story resonated far beyond the town's borders. Messages poured in from people who felt a connection to his journey, individuals grappling with their own invisible staircases, unseen struggles, and unspoken pain. Chantry, unintentionally, became a beacon of hope in a world accustomed to despair.

The once-skeptical town now embraced Chantry as a symbol of resilience. They organized events and gatherings, turning the invisible staircase into a makeshift pilgrimage site. For some, it was a quest for answers; for others, it offered a glimmer of hope in their darkest moments.

Chantry's life, once marked by rejection and solitude, now teemed with a sense of purpose. The invisible staircase, far from being a fleeting spectacle, had become a catalyst for change, not only for him but for those touched by his journey.

As Lydia continued to document Chantry's story, she, too, found herself transformed by the experience. The line between reporter and confidante blurred, and she became an unwitting participant in the unfolding narrative.

Together, Chantry and Lydia navigated the complexities of newfound fame, the evolving town dynamics, and the uncharted territory of the unseen realm. The invisible staircase, a mere metaphor for ascent, now symbolized the collective human struggle and the resilience found in the most unexpected places.

Chapter Three: Whispers Amongst the Stairs

The town continued to hum with energy, its streets pulsating with a newfound vibrancy. The invisible staircase had become a pilgrimage site, drawing people from neighboring towns and even distant cities. Chantry Chambers, now a reluctant figurehead, found himself at the epicenter of a growing movement.

One morning, as Chantry strolled through the town square, he heard snippets of conversations that echoed his own journey.

"Did you hear? A man in Chicago claims he found an invisible staircase too!"

"I read about it. They say it changes you, makes you see things differently."

Chantry couldn't escape the ripple effect of his ascent. The once-quiet town now buzzed with anticipation, its residents sharing stories of personal struggles and newfound hope.

As he passed by a local coffee shop, he caught sight of Lydia Turner immersed in conversation with a group of townspeople. The animated discussion seemed to revolve around the impact of the invisible staircase.

"Chantry, come join us!" Lydia beckoned with a warm smile, her eyes reflecting a genuine camaraderie that had developed between them.

Chantry hesitated but eventually joined the impromptu gathering. The eclectic group included people of different ages, backgrounds, and walks of life, all united by the invisible staircase.

Mabel, a spirited elderly woman with silver hair, clutched a cup of coffee as she shared her experience. "I never thought I'd find something like this at my age. It's like a second chance, you know?"

A young man named Jake, his eyes filled with youthful enthusiasm, chimed in, "It's like breaking free from the chains that held us down. We're not alone anymore."

Lydia, notebook in hand, guided the conversation, probing gently into the personal narratives that emerged. Chantry, though initially reserved, found solace in the shared stories. The invisible staircase, once a solitary journey, had woven a tapestry of interconnected lives.

As the sun dipped below the horizon, the group dispersed, leaving Chantry and Lydia alone in the fading light.

"It's incredible, isn't it?" Lydia remarked, her eyes reflecting a mix of wonder and fascination.

Chantry nodded, "I never expected this. The staircase was my escape, but it seems to have become something more."

Lydia, ever the investigative journalist, leaned forward, her eyes narrowing slightly. "Chantry, have you thought about what comes next? This has become a movement, a phenomenon. People are looking up to you."

Chantry sighed, his gaze drifting towards the invisible staircase etched in the evening sky. "I never planned for any of this. I just wanted to escape my pain. Now, it's as if the pain was a prerequisite for something greater."

Lydia nodded thoughtfully, "Maybe it's time to define your purpose, to give this movement direction. People are hungry for hope, for something to believe in. You have the chance to be a guiding light."

A mixture of apprehension and determination flickered in Chantry's eyes. "I'll consider it, Lydia. But I'm still figuring out what this all means for me."

The following days unfolded with a whirlwind of interviews, gatherings, and public appearances. Chantry became a reluctant symbol of resilience, his every word scrutinized for meaning. The invisible staircase, once a secret refuge, now stood as a beacon for those seeking solace and inspiration.

One evening, as Chantry stood on the outskirts of town, gazing at the staircase that disappeared into the sky, he found himself joined by a familiar presence—the crow that had accompanied him on that fateful journey.

"You again," Chantry muttered with a wry smile, sensing an unspoken connection between them.

The crow cawed, its dark feathers shimmering in the moonlight. Chantry felt a strange kinship with the creature, as if they shared a silent understanding.

The next morning, Chantry and Lydia gathered in a quaint bookstore on the town's main street. The shelves were filled with books on spirituality, self-discovery, and the inexplicable.

A group of locals, inspired by Chantry's journey, had organized a book club to explore these themes together.

As the discussion unfolded, diverse perspectives emerged. Some saw the invisible staircase as a spiritual awakening, while others approached it from a scientific or philosophical standpoint. The collective exploration became a catalyst for deeper connections and understanding.

Chantry, though initially reserved, found himself opening up about the emotions that had driven him to the staircase. Lydia observed the transformation in him, the once-burdened man now embracing his role in the unfolding narrative.

As the book club continued to meet, Chantry and Lydia embarked on a collaborative project. They decided to document the stories of those touched by the invisible staircase, creating a collective narrative that transcended individual experiences.

Their journey took them to neighboring towns, where they encountered people grappling with their own invisible staircases—metaphorical or otherwise. The movement sparked conversations about resilience, self-discovery, and the shared human experience.

Amidst the whirlwind of interviews and travels, Chantry's purpose became clearer. The invisible staircase was not just his salvation; it was a catalyst for collective healing and growth. The town that once rejected him now embraced him as a symbol of hope.

As Chantry and Lydia delved deeper into the unseen realm, their partnership evolved beyond journalistic collaboration. They became intertwined in the very fabric of the movement they sought to understand. The invisible staircase, once an escape, now beckoned them to explore the uncharted territories of human potential.

Chapter Four: Whispers of the Unknown

The invisible staircase had become a phenomenon that transcended the boundaries of the small town. Its influence rippled through the collective consciousness, drawing seekers, skeptics, and adventurers alike. Chantry Chambers and Lydia Turner, now partners in both life and exploration, found themselves at the forefront of this uncharted territory.

Driven by the whispers of the unknown, Chantry and Lydia embarked on a journey to unravel the mysteries that surrounded the invisible staircase. They received invitations from universities, research institutions, and even clandestine organizations, all eager to understand the supernatural phenomenon that had captivated the world.

Their first stop was the Institute for Paranormal Studies, nestled in the heart of a sprawling metropolis. Dr. Evelyn Blackwood, a renowned parapsychologist, greeted them with a mix of skepticism and genuine curiosity.

"Chantry, Lydia, welcome. I must admit, your story is unlike anything we've encountered in our research," Dr. Blackwood remarked, leading them through a labyrinth of corridors lined with shelves of arcane artifacts and paranormal paraphernalia.

The institute, despite its eccentric atmosphere, housed brilliant minds dedicated to unraveling the mysteries that blurred the lines between science and the supernatural. Chantry and Lydia, now accustomed to the attention, faced a battery of tests and experiments designed to explore the nature of the invisible staircase.

In a dimly lit chamber filled with humming machinery, Chantry stood on a platform surrounded by sensors. Dr. Blackwood monitored the readings, her eyes narrowing as the data defied conventional explanation.

"It's as if the very fabric of reality is bending around him," she murmured, studying the monitors.

Lydia, watching from a control room, exchanged glances with Chantry. The experience, once deeply personal, had evolved into a scientific enigma that fascinated and confounded even the experts.

As the experiments unfolded, Chantry's senses heightened. Whispers of distant echoes and unseen energies danced on the periphery of his awareness. He felt a connection to something beyond comprehension, a force that beckoned him to explore the uncharted realms of existence.

The Institute for Paranormal Studies became a hub of activity, attracting scholars, researchers, and enthusiasts from around the world. The invisible staircase, once a local secret, had become a global phenomenon.

Amidst the scientific scrutiny, Chantry and Lydia discovered an unexpected ally—Gideon Locke, a brilliant astrophysicist with a penchant for exploring the boundaries of reality. Locke, drawn by the allure of the invisible staircase, joined forces with them to unravel the cosmic mysteries that surrounded their journey.

Together, the trio delved into the realms of quantum physics, metaphysics, and ancient wisdom. They studied ancient texts, consulted with mystics, and embarked on daring experiments that pushed the boundaries of human understanding.

One evening, as they gathered in the heart of the institute's research chamber, a surge of energy rippled through the air. The invisible staircase, responding to an unseen force, manifested before them—a shimmering cascade of ethereal steps suspended in the void.

Gideon, his eyes ablaze with scientific curiosity, exclaimed, "This is beyond anything we've ever imagined. It's a doorway to another dimension, a bridge between the known and the unknown."

Chantry, sensing a deeper connection, stepped onto the staircase. The familiar sensation of ascent coursed through him, but this time, it resonated with a cosmic harmony that transcended earthly boundaries.

Lydia, her journalistic instincts merging with an insatiable curiosity, followed suit. Gideon, driven by the pursuit of knowledge, joined them on the invisible ascent.

As they climbed the ethereal steps, the fabric of reality seemed to warp and twist. Time became a fluid entity, and the boundaries between past, present, and future blurred into a kaleidoscopic dance of possibilities.

They emerged into a realm bathed in iridescent light—a cosmic tapestry that unfolded before their eyes. Celestial bodies, unknown constellations, and ethereal energies pulsed in harmony with the whispers of the unknown.

"This is incredible," Gideon murmured, his scientific mind grappling with the sheer magnitude of the spectacle.

Chantry, immersed in the cosmic resonance, felt a profound connection to the unseen forces that guided their journey. The invisible staircase, now a conduit to the cosmic unknown, beckoned them to explore the mysteries that lay beyond the edges of perception.

As they traversed the celestial expanse, encountering cosmic anomalies and unlocking the secrets of existence, Chantry and his companions realized that the invisible staircase was not just a physical ascent—it was a metaphysical journey that transcended the limitations of human understanding.

Chapter Five: Cosmic Revelations

The celestial expanse unfolded before Chantry, Lydia, and Gideon as they stood on the ethereal steps of the invisible staircase. The cosmic tapestry, painted with hues of unimaginable brilliance, beckoned them to explore the mysteries that lay beyond the edges of perception.

Gideon, his scientific curiosity ablaze, scanned the cosmic tableau with wide-eyed wonder. "This is beyond anything I've ever encountered in astrophysics. It's as if we've stepped into a living, breathing cosmic canvas."

Chantry, attuned to the unseen forces that guided their journey, felt a profound connection to the celestial energies that pulsed around them. "It's more than just a canvas,

Gideon. It's a symphony of existence, a dance of cosmic forces that defy our understanding."

Lydia, her journalistic instincts merging with an insatiable curiosity, gazed into the cosmic abyss. "Imagine the stories that could be told about this place, the narratives hidden within the fabric of the universe itself."

As they navigated the celestial expanse, encountering radiant nebulae, cosmic phenomena, and celestial beings that defied earthly description, the trio realized that the invisible staircase was a gateway to realms where reality intertwined with the metaphysical.

"I never thought the universe could be so... alive," Gideon murmured, his scientific skepticism giving way to awe.

Chantry, a smile playing on his lips, responded, "Science and mysticism aren't mutually exclusive, Gideon. This is a convergence of the known and the unknown, a bridge between what we understand and what lies beyond."

Their journey through the cosmic unknown brought moments of exhilaration and profound introspection. They encountered celestial beings who communicated through intricate patterns of light, witnessed the birth and death of stars, and traversed through dimensions where time itself seemed to dance to an ancient rhythm.

As they delved deeper into the cosmic tapestry, they discovered a celestial council—an assembly of wise beings who existed outside the constraints of space and time. The council, comprised of beings that embodied the essence of the universe, welcomed them with a harmonious resonance.

"We've been watching your journey, Chantry Chambers. Your ascent on the invisible staircase has opened a doorway to realms seldom explored by mortals," intoned a celestial being, its form shifting between radiant energy and profound wisdom.

Lydia, her journalistic instincts ignited, couldn't contain her excitement. "Who are you? What is the purpose of this cosmic tapestry?"

The celestial council responded in unison, their voices echoing through the cosmic void. "We are the stewards of cosmic balance, the custodians of the tapestry that weaves through the fabric of existence. The invisible staircase serves as a bridge between realms, a conduit for those who seek to explore the interconnectedness of all things."

Chantry, humbled by the presence of these cosmic beings, asked, "What is the purpose of our journey? Why were we chosen to traverse these celestial realms?"

The celestial beings emanated a radiant energy, conveying a profound truth. "Chantry Chambers, Lydia Turner, Gideon Locke, your journey is a testament to the resilience of the human spirit. The invisible staircase is a gift, a path that leads to self-discovery and enlightenment. You have bridged the gap between worlds, and in doing so, you've become catalysts for cosmic revelations."

As the cosmic council imparted their wisdom, the trio felt a surge of energy—an infusion of cosmic knowledge that transcended language and comprehension. They glimpsed the interconnectedness of all things, the universal symphony that echoed through every atom and every heartbeat.

In a moment of cosmic clarity, Lydia exclaimed, "We are not alone in the universe, and our existence is part of a grand narrative that extends beyond the boundaries of our understanding."

Gideon, overwhelmed by the revelations, added, "The invisible staircase is a conduit for collective evolution, a cosmic invitation for humanity to explore the vastness of the unknown."

The celestial council, their radiant presence fading, echoed a parting message. "Go forth, explorers of the cosmic unknown. Your journey has just begun, and the revelations you seek are intertwined with the destiny of the universe itself."

As Chantry, Lydia, and Gideon descended the invisible staircase, their minds teeming with newfound cosmic knowledge, they felt a profound sense of purpose. The cosmic revelations had opened a door to infinite possibilities, and the adventure continued

beyond the celestial expanse.

Chapter Six: The Global Ascent

News of the cosmic revelations experienced by Chantry, Lydia, and Gideon spread like wildfire across the world. The invisible staircase, once a local enigma, now captivated the collective imagination, igniting a global quest for cosmic exploration.

As the trio returned from their celestial journey, the phenomenon manifested anew. Invisible staircases began to appear in diverse corners of the globe, sparking curiosity, wonder, and a shared sense of awe. The cosmic revelations were no longer confined to a small town—they had become a global phenomenon.

Reports flooded in from major cities, remote landscapes, and ancient sites, all describing the emergence of invisible staircases that defied conventional explanation. Governments, scientists, and spiritual leaders grappled with the implications of this transcendent phenomenon, while people from all walks of life embarked on their own journeys of ascent.

In New York City, a staircase materialized amidst the towering skyscrapers of Manhattan, drawing the attention of urban explorers, artists, and seekers of the extraordinary. The bustling metropolis became a canvas for the convergence of cosmic energy and human curiosity.

In the heart of the Amazon rainforest, an invisible staircase emerged, intertwining with the vibrant tapestry of biodiversity. Indigenous communities, guided by ancient wisdom, saw the stairway as a bridge between the earthly realms and the celestial unknown.

On the plains of Africa, a majestic staircase rose from the savannah, inviting nomadic tribes and wildlife to coexist in the dance of cosmic exploration. The invisible staircases became conduits for shared experiences, connecting people from different cultures and backgrounds.

In the Himalayas, where spirituality and mysticism intersected with the towering peaks, a staircase appeared, challenging monks and ascetics to embark on a celestial pilgrimage. The sacred mountains echoed with the chants of those who sought higher truths.

As the invisible staircases proliferated, the world witnessed a global renaissance of exploration, connection, and self-discovery. The phenomenon defied geopolitical borders, cultural differences, and scientific paradigms. It became a testament to the universal human yearning for connection with something greater than themselves.

Chantry, Lydia, and Gideon, recognizing the transformative power of the invisible staircases, became ambassadors of cosmic exploration. They traveled the world, sharing their experiences, facilitating dialogues, and fostering a global community united by the pursuit of cosmic truths.

In the midst of this global ascent, the trio encountered individuals whose stories mirrored their own—a spectrum of seekers, skeptics, and dreamers who embraced the invisible staircases as portals to a new era of understanding.

In a bustling market in Tokyo, Chantry engaged in a conversation with Hiroshi, a physicist intrigued by the intersection of science and mysticism. "These staircases challenge our understanding of reality. What if they are glimpses into dimensions that exist beyond the limits of our perception?"

Lydia, interviewing a group of indigenous elders in Australia, listened to their ancient tales of Dreamtime. "The invisible staircases are like the song lines of the cosmos, connecting us to the celestial stories written in the stars."

Gideon, collaborating with a team of astronomers in Chile, observed the cosmic alignments of the staircases. "It's as if the universe itself is communicating with us through these celestial pathways. There's a cosmic language waiting to be deciphered."

The global ascent became a transformative journey for humanity—one that transcended cultural divides, philosophical differences, and the constraints of ordinary reality. The invisible staircases, now a symbol of collective evolution, urged people to look beyond the mundane and reach for the cosmic unknown.

Chapter Seven: Ascension or Apocalypse

As the invisible staircases continued to proliferate across the globe, a diverse array of reactions ensued. While many embraced the cosmic revelations as a source of unity and exploration, a fringe of radical religious groups interpreted the phenomenon as a harbinger of the end times.

In a small town in the southern United States, a charismatic preacher named Ezekiel Stone rallied his congregation around the belief that the invisible staircases were a divine signal, marking the imminent apocalypse. The fervent preacher, eyes ablaze with conviction, declared,

"These stairways are the celestial bridges leading us to the final judgment. Prepare, brethren, for the reckoning is upon us!"

Stone's followers, donned in white robes adorned with cryptic symbols, gathered in a makeshift compound on the outskirts of town. They fervently awaited their ascension to the heavens, convinced that the invisible staircases were portals to a divine realm where only the chosen would find salvation.

Chantry, Lydia, and Gideon, having caught wind of Stone's zealous movement, felt compelled to investigate. They arrived in the small town, where an air of tension hung thick amidst the fervent whispers of impending doom.

Stone, a commanding figure with a wild mane of silver hair, greeted the trio with a fervent smile. "Welcome, wanderers! The cosmic revelations have foretold your arrival. Join us in preparing for the ascension or face the consequences of divine judgment."

Lydia, ever the investigative journalist, probed, "What makes you so certain that these staircases lead to the end of the world? We've seen their beauty and connection to the cosmos."

Stone, his eyes ablaze with conviction, replied, "Beauty can be deceiving, my friends. These staircases are the bridges to a realm where the righteous will ascend, leaving behind the sinful to face the celestial wrath. It is the grand finale of our existence."

As the group explored the makeshift compound, they encountered fervent followers who spoke of impending doom with a mix of fear and anticipation. Stone's charismatic sermons echoed through the air, stirring the emotions of those who sought refuge in the promise of ascension.

Chantry, sensing the dangerous fervor building, spoke to a young woman named Abigail, who seemed torn between doubt and loyalty. "Abigail, is this truly the only path to salvation? The invisible staircases have brought wonder and unity to the world, not destruction."

Abigail, her eyes filled with uncertainty, whispered, "I don't know what to believe anymore. Stone has a way of making it all seem so real, like we're on the brink of something extraordinary."

Meanwhile, Gideon engaged in a conversation with Stone, attempting to understand the source of his convictions. "Ezekiel, we've seen the beauty of the cosmic tapestry. Why interpret it as a precursor to apocalypse? Can't it be a call to collective enlightenment?"

Stone, unwavering in his beliefs, responded with fervor, "Enlightenment is a luxury for those who can afford it. The invisible staircases are not a blessing but a test. Only those who heed the call of ascension will find redemption."

As the tension escalated within the compound, the town, unaware of the impending crisis, continued to explore their own invisible staircases with a sense of wonder and curiosity. The global ascent, marked by diverse perspectives, now faced a looming challenge—

one that threatened to fracture the delicate balance between cosmic exploration and apocalyptic fervor.

Chapter Eight: Bridges of Unity

As the tension within the small town intensified, Chantry, Lydia, and Gideon found themselves at the heart of a growing divide. The charismatic preacher Ezekiel Stone continued to rally his followers, prophesying the impending apocalypse as the invisible staircases multiplied across the world.

Chantry, having faced rejection and prejudice throughout his life, saw an opportunity to use his newfound fame as a voice for unity. He embarked on a mission to bridge the gap between the diverse perspectives emerging in the wake of the invisible staircases.

In a global press conference, Chantry shared his personal journey and the transformative power of the invisible staircases. His voice, resonating with authenticity and vulnerability, reached millions around the world.

"People of Earth," Chantry began, his words carried on waves of sincerity, "I stand before you as someone who knows what it's like to feel invisible, to be judged for who you are. But these invisible staircases, they're not here to divide us. They're a call for unity, understanding, and acceptance."

Chantry's message gained momentum, drawing support from individuals across cultures, religions, and walks of life. His influence extended beyond the LGBTQ community, becoming a beacon of hope for those seeking common ground amidst the chaos.

In the small town, where Stone's influence loomed large, Chantry organized a town hall meeting. With a diverse panel representing different perspectives, including religious leaders, scientists, and members of the LGBTQ community, the meeting aimed to foster dialogue and dispel the fear that Stone's prophecies had instilled.

Stone, skeptical of Chantry's intentions, attended the meeting with his followers in tow.

The town hall became a battleground of ideologies, but Chantry stood firm in his commitment to unity.

"Friends, we may have different beliefs, but we share this planet, and these invisible staircases are a gift, not a curse. Let's embrace the opportunity to learn from one another, to build bridges of understanding," Chantry implored.

Lydia, as the moderator, facilitated a respectful exchange of ideas. The religious leaders spoke of faith and humility, the scientists highlighted the marvels of cosmic exploration, and Chantry emphasized the importance of love and acceptance.

Gideon, using his background in diplomacy, addressed Stone directly. "Ezekiel, the world is at a crossroads. We can either let fear and division define us, or we can choose unity and understanding. The invisible staircases are not a threat but a chance for humanity to evolve together."

The town hall meeting, broadcasted globally, became a symbol of hope. Chantry's message resonated, prompting people to reassess their fears and prejudices. As the world watched, the small town, once on the brink of division, became a microcosm of a potential global reconciliation.

Chapter Nine: The Celestial Reckoning

As the world grappled with the unfolding drama surrounding the invisible staircases, a new energy permeated the global consciousness. The small town's journey towards unity had ignited a spark that resonated far beyond its borders. People began to reevaluate their beliefs, question their fears, and seek connection rather than division.

Chantry's influence continued to grow, reaching corners of the world where acceptance and understanding were most needed. He used his platform not only to bridge the gaps between different communities but also to inspire acts of kindness and compassion. The hashtag #StairwayToUnity trended across social media platforms, becoming a symbol of the collective journey towards a better world.

In a bustling metropolis halfway across the globe, a diverse group of individuals gathered at the base of an invisible staircase that had materialized in the heart of the city. The group, representing various ethnicities, religions, and backgrounds, looked up at the ethereal structure with a mix of curiosity and anticipation.

Among them was Anisa, a young Muslim woman who had faced discrimination for wearing a hijab. Standing next to her was Javier, a gay artist who had battled prejudice in the art world. The group also included Dr. Mei Lin, a brilliant scientist, and Raj, a charismatic community leader.

Chantry, Lydia, and Gideon arrived to witness this diverse assembly of individuals who had come together under the banner of unity. Anisa, with a smile that reflected both resilience and hope, stepped forward and spoke.

"For too long, we've been divided by our differences. But these invisible staircases remind us that our similarities are greater than our disparities. Let's ascend together, not in fear, but in celebration of our shared humanity."

The group, hand in hand, began to ascend the staircase, symbolizing a collective step towards unity. As they climbed, the celestial energy of the staircase responded, shimmering with colors that mirrored the diversity of the group. The air hummed with a harmonious melody, and the city below, with its skyscrapers and bustling streets, faded into a distant memory.

At the summit, the group found themselves in a surreal landscape, bathed in a cosmic glow. It was a place where judgments melted away, and the barriers between them dissolved. Anisa and Javier exchanged stories, realizing the common threads that wove through their diverse experiences.

Dr. Mei Lin, inspired by the celestial energy, contemplated the mysteries of the universe. "Perhaps these staircases are not just physical pathways but conduits for a higher understanding—a language that transcends our limited perspectives."

Raj, gazing into the cosmic expanse, added, "In this celestial realm, we are not defined by our labels or backgrounds. We are beings connected by the same cosmic energy that flows through the universe."

Chantry, Lydia, and Gideon, witnessing the transformative power of unity, felt a profound sense of fulfillment. The invisible staircases, once symbols of cosmic exploration, had become bridges connecting hearts and minds across the world.

As the diverse group descended from the celestial summit, they carried with them a shared vision of a more compassionate world. The hashtag #StairwayToUnity gained momentum, inspiring countless others to embrace the transformative journey towards understanding, acceptance, and love.

Chapter Ten: Shadows in the Cosmos

As the global movement towards unity gained momentum, a shadowy force began to stir in the cosmic tapestry. Unbeknownst to the world, a clandestine organization, calling themselves the "Cosmic Purifiers," emerged with a sinister agenda to exploit the celestial phenomena for their own gain.

Chantry, Lydia, and Gideon, who had become the unofficial ambassadors of the invisible staircases, received a cryptic message hinting at a dark force manipulating the cosmic energies. Determined to uncover the truth, they embarked on a journey to the heart of the cosmic anomalies.

Their quest led them to a hidden facility nestled deep within a desolate landscape. The air crackled with an eerie energy as they approached, sensing that they were on the precipice of a revelation. The entrance to the facility, disguised as a nondescript building, concealed the true nature of the Cosmic Purifiers' operations.

Inside, they discovered a vast network of scientists, engineers, and covert operatives working in tandem to harness the cosmic energies emanating from the invisible staircases. The leader, a shadowy figure known only as Helios, revealed their twisted vision for humanity.

"Behold the culmination of our efforts!" Helios exclaimed, gesturing towards a colossal machine that siphoned the celestial energy. "We intend to weaponize this power, ensuring dominance over all who oppose us. The staircases are not conduits for unity; they are tools for supremacy."

Chantry, outraged by the betrayal of the cosmic gift, confronted Helios. "You're perverting the very essence of what these staircases represent. Unity, understanding, and compassion—not domination!"

Lydia, utilizing her investigative prowess, accessed the facility's data archives. Shockingly, she discovered plans to manipulate the cosmic energies to create a destructive force capable of subjugating entire nations. The Cosmic Purifiers aimed to exploit the staircases for their own sinister agenda.

Gideon, sensing the urgency of the situation, initiated a daring plan to disable the cosmic weapon. The trio navigated the labyrinthine facility, evading security measures and overcoming obstacles designed to protect the insidious project.

As they reached the heart of the operation, a tense confrontation ensued between Chantry, Lydia, Gideon, and Helios. The celestial energy crackled in the air, mirroring the escalating conflict between the forces of unity and those seeking cosmic domination.

With a surge of determination, Gideon managed to disable the machine just as it reached its critical phase. The cosmic energies, once harnessed for malevolent purposes, surged uncontrollably, creating a dazzling display that illuminated the entire facility.

Amidst the chaos, Helios attempted to escape, but Chantry intercepted him. "You've underestimated the power of unity," Chantry declared, his eyes ablaze with cosmic energy. With a forceful gesture, he neutralized Helios, rendering him powerless.

As the facility crumbled, Lydia, Chantry, and Gideon narrowly escaped the impending destruction. They emerged into the open air, witnessing the cosmic energies dispersing into the atmosphere, no longer tainted by the dark ambitions of the Cosmic Purifiers.

Chapter Eleven: Confronting Shadows

In the aftermath of their victory against the Cosmic Purifiers, Chantry, Lydia, and Gideon found themselves traversing through a city vibrant with newfound hope. The celestial energies, once tainted by malevolence, now bathed the world in a gentle glow, serving as a testament to the triumph of unity over darkness.

As Chantry became a symbol of the global movement towards understanding and acceptance, he also became a target for those who perceived the invisible staircases as a threat. In a city where shadows still clung to the edges, a group known as "The Purity Protectors" emerged, denouncing Chantry as a harbinger of evil.

One evening, as Chantry addressed a diverse crowd gathered at a public square, The Purity Protectors staged a vehement protest. Clad in dark attire, their banners adorned with hateful slogans, they chanted slogans that reverberated through the air like discordant notes in a symphony of progress.

Gideon, ever vigilant, noticed the growing tension. He whispered to Chantry, "We need to be careful. These people are fueled by fear and ignorance."

Chantry, though accustomed to adversity, felt a pang of discomfort as he faced the hostile group. Lydia, always ready to document events, discreetly recorded the unfolding confrontation.

The leader of The Purity Protectors, a charismatic but venomous figure named Malachi, approached Chantry with an air of self-righteousness. "You claim to bring unity, but your actions are nothing but a sinister plot to destroy our way of life. We won't let your corrupted influence poison our society."

Chantry, keeping his composure, responded, "I come in peace, seeking understanding and acceptance for all. The staircases are not tools of destruction but bridges connecting us. Can't you see that?"

Malachi, unmoved by Chantry's words, raised his voice, inciting the crowd further. "This abomination preaches deception! We must stand against the darkness he brings. Our purity will prevail!"

The confrontation escalated, and the crowd, torn between curiosity and hostility, formed a tense divide. Chantry, determined to defuse the situation, addressed the onlookers with a resolute tone. "I understand your fears, but let's not succumb to hate. We can find common ground and build a future where everyone is accepted for who they are."

Lydia's camera captured the fervent exchange, documenting the clash of ideologies that echoed the broader struggles of society.

Gideon, positioned strategically, remained vigilant, ready to intervene if the situation spiraled out of control.

In the midst of the heated debate, a young girl, no older than twelve, stepped forward from the crowd. Her eyes, wide with innocence, held a curious glint as she looked up at Chantry.

"Why are they so angry at you?" she asked, sincerity cutting through the cacophony.

Chantry, bending down to her level, responded, "Sometimes people fear what they don't understand. But we can change that. Together."

The innocence in the girl's question struck a chord, prompting a ripple of contemplation among the crowd. The Purity Protectors, momentarily silenced, faced the reflection of their actions in the eyes of a child.

As the confrontation reached a fragile equilibrium, Chantry extended a hand, not as a gesture of superiority but as an invitation to dialogue. The shadows of prejudice confronted the light of understanding, and the outcome remained uncertain.

Chapter Twelve: Bridges of Understanding

The public square echoed with the tension of conflicting ideologies as Chantry faced the leader of The Purity Protectors, Malachi. The crowd stood divided, with curious onlookers caught between the polarizing forces of acceptance and fear. In the midst of the charged atmosphere, one member of The Purity Protectors, a young man named Ethan, found himself wrestling with an internal struggle.

As the verbal sparring continued, Ethan, standing on the fringes of the crowd, watched with a mixture of uncertainty and curiosity. His internal conflict mirrored the tumultuous clash of beliefs unfolding before him.

Chantry, recognizing the internal struggle within Ethan, directed a portion of his words towards him. "Ethan, isn't it time to question the walls that divide us? We all share the same planet, breathe the same air. Let's find common ground instead of perpetuating hatred."

Ethan, torn between loyalty to his group and a burgeoning desire for understanding, took a hesitant step forward. His eyes, filled with both doubt and curiosity, met Chantry's gaze.

"Chantry is right," he continued, his voice carrying over the square. "Let's not define ourselves by the fears that others impose on us. We have the power to change, to build bridges instead of walls."

Ethan, feeling the weight of Chantry's words, looked around at the faces in the crowd. His internal struggle intensified as he grappled with the teachings of The Purity Protectors and the yearning for a different perspective.

Gideon, watching the dynamics unfold, approached Ethan with a gentle demeanor. "It's never too late to question the beliefs that hold us captive. Understanding starts with a willingness to listen and learn."

Amidst the charged atmosphere, Chantry extended an olive branch to Ethan, inviting him to engage in open dialogue. "Ethan, I believe in the capacity for change within every individual. Let's bridge the gap between us."

In that moment of vulnerability, Ethan hesitated but took a courageous step towards Chantry. The crowd, hushed in anticipation, witnessed the potential for transformation.

As Chantry and Ethan engaged in a heartfelt conversation, their exchange transcended the boundaries of ideology. Chantry shared stories of his own struggles, the pain of rejection, and the journey towards self-discovery. Ethan, in turn, began to unravel the layers of indoctrination that had shaped his beliefs.

The square, once a battleground of opposing forces, became a canvas for the subtle art of understanding. The two individuals, seemingly worlds apart, discovered the common threads that connected their humanity.

Days turned into weeks, and Ethan's perspective gradually shifted. The initial animosity evolved into a profound connection, as he and Chantry explored the invisible staircases together, stepping into realms of self-discovery and shared experiences.

Chapter Thirteen: Love in the Air

As Chantry and Ethan continued their journey of self-discovery, the invisible staircases became not just conduits of connection but pathways to something more profound. The initial sparks of understanding between them blossomed into a genuine and unexpected connection, challenging the preconceived notions that had shaped their lives.

Their shared experiences, from climbing invisible staircases to engaging in heartfelt conversations, deepened the bond between Chantry and Ethan. What began as a journey of understanding transformed into a voyage of love, defying societal expectations and transcending the barriers that had initially divided them.

In the quiet moments shared between steps, Chantry found himself drawn to Ethan's warmth, his kindness, and the courage it took to question the beliefs he had held for so long. Likewise, Ethan discovered a profound sense of acceptance and belonging in Chantry's company, a feeling that had eluded him in the rigid world of The Purity Protectors.

One evening, beneath the canvas of a starlit sky, Chantry confessed to Gideon, "I never thought I'd find love amidst these invisible staircases. Love wasn't part of the plan, but here I am, falling."

Gideon, with a knowing smile, replied, "Love has a way of finding us when we least expect it. Embrace it, Chantry. It's a force that can change the world."

As Chantry and Ethan's love deepened, so did their impact on the world around them. News of their transformative journey spread, captivating the hearts and minds of people far beyond their immediate surroundings. The story of an LGBTQ advocate and a former member of The Purity Protectors finding love became a beacon of hope in a world yearning for connection and understanding.

Their love story transcended borders, resonating with individuals who had felt marginalized, rejected, or confined by societal norms. The invisible staircases, once symbols of personal growth, now became conduits for a universal message of love, acceptance, and the power of human connection.

Chantry and Ethan, aware of the responsibility that their newfound love carried, took to the global stage. They shared their story through interviews, documentaries, and public appearances, igniting conversations about acceptance, love, and the transformative potential within each individual.

Their journey became a movement—a movement not just for LGBTQ rights, but for the rights of all individuals to love and be loved without judgment. The world, once divided by invisible walls of prejudice, began to crumble as Chantry and Ethan's love became a catalyst for change.

Chapter Fourteen: Celestial Connection

In the soft glow of moonlight, Chantry and Ethan found themselves on the highest step of an invisible staircase, their love illuminated by the stars that surrounded them. The air hummed with a quiet intensity, a palpable energy that mirrored the depth of their emotions.

As they stood there, hand in hand, their connection transcended the physical realm. Chantry's heart, once heavy with the weight of rejection, now beat in harmony with Ethan's. They shared a silent understanding that words could never capture—the unspoken language of two souls entwined.

Ethan looked into Chantry's eyes, his gaze a mixture of vulnerability and desire. "Chantry, I never thought I'd find love like this. It's as if the universe conspired to bring us together."

Chantry, his heart overflowing with emotion, whispered, "Love has a way of rewriting our stories. We've climbed invisible staircases, defied gravity, and found each other. Let's embrace this moment, Ethan."

Their lips met in a gentle kiss, a celestial dance that mirrored the stars above. Time seemed to stand still as they explored the uncharted territory of each other's hearts. The world faded away, leaving only the echo of their shared breaths and the beating of their entwined hearts.

Their love scene unfolded like a cosmic ballet, a dance of passion and intimacy beneath the cosmic canopy. Their connection was a symphony of sensations, each touch and caress a note in the melody of their shared desires.

Meanwhile, on Earth, the geopolitical landscape took an unexpected turn. In a misguided attempt to control the perceived threat of the invisible staircases, Iran and Pakistan joined forces, targeting the USA with a series of cyber-attacks. Fearful of the unknown and driven by paranoia, they sought to eliminate what they perceived as a potential danger to global stability.

The world teetered on the edge of chaos as Chantry and Ethan, unaware of the unfolding events, continued their celestial dance. Love, a force that transcended boundaries, seemed to be the only antidote to the escalating tensions on Earth.

As Chantry and Ethan embraced their connection, their love became a beacon of hope amidst the uncertainty. Little did they know that their journey, intertwined with the invisible staircases, would play a pivotal role in reshaping the destiny of not just their lives, but the fate of the world.

Chapter Fifteen: Diplomacy of the Heart

Amidst the cosmic embrace of the invisible staircases, Chantry and Ethan were caught in the euphoria of their celestial connection when an unexpected intrusion disrupted their sanctuary. A sudden swirl of energy enveloped them, and before they could comprehend what was happening, they found themselves transported to a different reality.

As their surroundings shifted, Chantry and Ethan found themselves standing in a lavish room, adorned with the trappings of political power. The air carried a tense energy, and the soft hum of distant conversations hinted at the gravity of the situation.

Before them, the President of the United States stood with a stern expression. "Chantry, Ethan, welcome. I apologize for the abruptness, but we are facing a crisis that requires your unique perspective."

Confused and disoriented, Chantry asked, "What's happening? Where are we?"

The President, flanked by Secret Service agents, explained the dire situation unfolding on Earth. "Iran and Pakistan have initiated cyber-attacks, fueled by paranoia about the invisible staircases. They believe it's a threat, and tensions are escalating toward the use of nuclear weapons."

Ethan, realizing the gravity of the situation, interjected, "But why us? What can we do?"

The President's gaze softened. "Your story, your journey, has become a symbol of hope and unity. We believe your presence, your ability to bridge gaps, can help us avert a global catastrophe. The Middle East is on the brink, and we need your help to show them that love and understanding can triumph over fear."

Chantry and Ethan exchanged glances, recognizing the weight of the responsibility thrust upon them. With a shared nod, they agreed to lend their voices to a cause greater than themselves.

The Secret Service agents escorted Chantry and Ethan to a secure location where they could communicate with leaders from the Middle

East. The video conference bridged the physical gap, connecting hearts and minds across continents.

Chantry, his voice resonating with sincerity, addressed the leaders, "We understand your fears, your concerns. But we've experienced something extraordinary—something beyond the realm of what we once believed. Love has the power to unite, to dispel fear, and to create a future where differences can coexist."

Ethan, drawing from his own transformation, added, "We've seen the beauty that lies beyond the walls of prejudice. The invisible staircases, a manifestation of our shared humanity, have shown us that we are all connected. Let us find a way to build bridges instead of launching missiles."

The leaders, their expressions shifting from skepticism to contemplation, listened to Chantry and Ethan's impassioned plea. The universal language of love, transcending borders and ideologies, began to weave its magic through the airwaves.

As the conversation unfolded, the once rigid stance of the Middle Eastern leaders softened. The fear that had gripped their hearts started to yield to the possibility of a different future—

one where understanding prevailed over hostility.

Chantry and Ethan's diplomacy of the heart, coupled with the President's diplomatic efforts, became a turning point in the global crisis. Love, the invisible thread that connected them all, emerged as the catalyst for change.

Chapter Sixteen: The Tenuous Thread

Chantry and Ethan, propelled into the heart of a geopolitical maelstrom, found themselves aboard a diplomatic flight to the Middle East. The world outside the airplane windows seemed to writhe with uncertainty, as if the fabric of reality itself was fraying at the seams. The news broadcast on the in-flight monitors painted a picture of escalating chaos, with nations on the brink of catastrophic decisions.

Upon their arrival, Chantry and Ethan were ushered into a dimly lit room where leaders from Iran and Pakistan awaited them. Tension hung in the air like a heavy fog, and the stern expressions of the leaders hinted at the gravity of the situation.

The Iranian President, his voice edged with suspicion, addressed Chantry and Ethan, "You claim these invisible staircases are a force of love and unity. Yet, our people fear them, and we cannot ignore the potential threat they pose."

Ethan, undeterred by the palpable tension, responded, "We understand your concerns. Fear often blinds us to possibilities beyond our comprehension. Let us explain the true nature of the staircases and how they symbolize unity, not a threat."

As the conversation unfolded, emotions ran high. The leaders remained skeptical, their mistrust etched on their faces. The air crackled with tension, and at one point, guns were drawn by security forces on both sides.

Chantry, with a calm yet determined voice, implored, "Please, we are not your enemies. We've seen the transformative power of love on our journey. Let us share this understanding with you, let us find common ground."

Ethan, drawing upon their experiences, continued, "The staircases are not a weapon. They are a bridge between worlds, a testament to the shared humanity that binds us all. Let us build bridges instead of walls, understanding instead of animosity."

As the leaders listened, the atmosphere began to shift. The initial hostility began to wane, replaced by a reluctant curiosity. The guns were holstered, and a fragile truce settled over the room.

Chantry, seizing the opportunity, recounted their journey, the challenges they faced, and the transformative moments that occurred on the invisible staircases. He spoke of love, acceptance, and the power of unity to overcome even the deepest divides.

The Pakistani President, visibly moved, finally spoke, "Perhaps we have been too quick to judge. The world outside is unraveling, and we need solutions. Can these staircases truly bring people together?"

Ethan nodded, "Yes, they can. But we need to approach this with open hearts and minds. Let us work together to bridge the gaps, to find common ground and build a future where fear no longer dictates our actions."

The room, once a battleground of opposing ideologies, became a crucible for change. The leaders, initially driven by fear, began to see the potential for a different path—a path paved with understanding, compassion, and the transformative power of love.

Chapter Seventeen: A Symphony of Unity

As Chantry and Ethan successfully diffused the nuclear threat in the Middle East, the world watched in collective relief. The invisible staircases, once feared, now held the promise of a brighter future. The Iranian and Pakistani leaders, inspired by Chantry and Ethan's message of unity, chose to withdraw their nuclear weapons, marking a historic moment of de-escalation.

Returning to U.S. soil, Chantry and Ethan found themselves thrust into the spotlight once again. The President, recognizing their invaluable contribution to global peace, organized a press conference of unprecedented scale. It was more than a mere acknowledgment; it was a celebration of love triumphing over fear.

In a grand auditorium filled with dignitaries, journalists, and citizens from around the world, Chantry and Ethan stood alongside the President. The air buzzed with anticipation as the President took the stage, offering gratitude for the transformative power of love that had averted a global catastrophe.

"I stand here today with two extraordinary individuals who have shown us the way forward—a path illuminated by love, understanding, and the courage to bridge divides," the President declared, and the audience erupted in applause.

Chantry and Ethan, humbled by the enormity of the moment, exchanged glances before stepping forward to address the world. The President draped medals around their necks, symbolizing the recognition of their selfless efforts.

Chantry, with sincerity in his eyes, spoke first, "We are not heroes. We are just two individuals who, through an extraordinary journey, discovered that love has the power to change the world. This isn't about us; it's about all of us coming together."

Ethan, echoing the sentiment, added, "We've been given a gift—the invisible staircases—that revealed a truth we all need to embrace. We are more connected than we realize, and together, we can overcome any challenge."

The press conference, broadcast live across the globe, broke records with its viewership, surpassing even the most-watched events in history. The world, hungry for a message of hope, tuned in to witness the unfolding narrative of unity and transformation.

As the accolades continued to pour in, Chantry and Ethan gracefully accepted the honors, always redirecting the attention to the larger message they carried. They spoke of the interconnectedness of humanity, the need for empathy, and the potential within each person to contribute to a better world.

The symbolic gesture of accepting medals turned into a symbolic gesture of collective responsibility. The world, witnessing this extraordinary moment, began to see the invisible staircases not as a threat but as a gift—a catalyst for change and unity.

Chapter Eighteen: A Lakeside Serenity

The wave of fame and glory that had swept over Chantry and Ethan seemed like a distant echo compared to the tranquility they craved. The media frenzy had settled, and the world, now aware of the invisible staircases' transformative potential, looked to them with admiration and respect. However, for Chantry and Ethan, the allure of a quiet life by the lake outweighed the allure of the global stage.

The couple found themselves drawn to a picturesque countryside, where a secluded house overlooked a serene lake. It was a place where the rustle of leaves and the gentle lapping of water against the shore created a symphony of nature—an antidote to the cacophony of the outside world.

As they settled into their new life, Chantry and Ethan reveled in the simple pleasures. The morning sun painting the sky in hues of pink and gold, the aroma of freshly brewed coffee, and the soft whispers of the wind through the trees became the backdrop of their days. It was a life they had always dreamed of—a life far removed from the spotlight that had briefly consumed them.

Yet, the echoes of the outside world persisted. Letters of gratitude poured in from people whose lives had been touched by their journey. The lake house became a sanctuary not only for Chantry and Ethan but also for those seeking solace and inspiration.

One day, as they sat on the porch, watching the sun dip below the horizon, a mysterious figure approached from the shadows. It was the crow, the same one that had guided Chantry on the invisible staircases.

"Chantry Chambers, Ethan Hunter," the crow spoke with an otherworldly resonance, "your journey is not yet complete. The world still yearns for the transformative touch of love and unity."

Chantry exchanged a glance with Ethan, recognizing the weight of the crow's words. Despite their desire for a quiet life, a higher purpose seemed to call them once again.

The crow continued, "The staircases are evolving, manifesting in ways unforeseen. Your role in this cosmic tapestry is not over. Embrace the gift you've been given, for the world still needs your guidance."

With those enigmatic words, the crow took flight, disappearing into the gathering dusk. Chantry and Ethan, though initially hesitant, felt a sense of duty stirring within them. The invisible staircases, it seemed, were not done with them yet.

Chapter Nineteen: The Unfolding Tapestry

The lakeside serenity held a tranquil rhythm for Chantry and Ethan, but the mysterious message from the crow lingered in the air like a whisper of fate. As they navigated the waters of their secluded lake in a small rowboat, the stillness of the surroundings heightened their contemplation.

Ethan dipped the oars into the water, creating gentle ripples that mirrored the intricate tapestry of their lives. Chantry, lost in thought, broke the silence. "Do you believe in destiny, Ethan?"

Ethan smiled, guiding the boat toward the heart of the lake. "I believe in us, Chantry. Destiny is just the name we give to the journey we embark on."

Their days by the lake unfolded like a chapter in a cherished novel. They embraced the quietude, savoring each moment as the invisible staircases continued to weave their influence across the world. The couple, although yearning for simplicity, couldn't ignore the pull of the unseen forces.

One morning, as they strolled along the lakeshore, the sky painted in hues of dawn, they encountered an anomaly—a shimmering staircase materializing before them. It was visible, tangible, unlike the ethereal staircases of their past.

Chantry touched the cool brass railing, and a surge of energy coursed through him. A vision flashed before his eyes—an intricate pattern connecting people, places, and stories. It was as if the staircase was a cosmic loom, weaving the threads of humanity into a tapestry of interconnected destinies.

Ethan, sensing the significance, placed his hand over Chantry's. "Where does it lead?"

The crow, perched on a nearby branch, cawed with an air of knowing. "To places unknown, yet familiar. To people waiting to discover the love that binds them."

Chantry and Ethan exchanged determined glances. The lakeside idyll had been a respite, but the call to action resonated in their hearts. They ascended the staircase, stepping into the unknown with a shared purpose—to continue the journey of spreading love, understanding, and unity.

As they climbed, the world below transformed. The lake and the tranquil house became a distant memory, replaced by a panorama of diverse landscapes and faces. The invisible staircases, once a personal odyssey, now unfolded into a global narrative, connecting hearts and minds across continents.

Chapter Twenty: Echoes of Eternity

Chantry and Ethan ascended the tangible staircase, stepping into realms beyond their imagination. Each step unveiled new vistas; each landing brought encounters with souls yearning for connection. The invisible staircases, once confined to the shadows, now manifested openly, revealing themselves to a world awakening to the power of unity.

Their journey took them to bustling cities, ancient temples, and serene meadows where whispers of love echoed through the air. As they climbed higher, the threads of their own story intertwined with those of countless others, weaving a tapestry of shared destinies.

One evening, on a staircase suspended between the clouds, Chantry and Ethan found themselves enveloped in a celestial glow. A cosmic symphony played in the background—a harmonious convergence of diverse voices and cultures. The crow, their ethereal guide, soared alongside them, its feathers shimmering with an otherworldly light.

"You've become conduits of change," the crow cawed, its voice resonating through the heavens. "But your ultimate purpose awaits at the zenith of these staircases."

As they reached a landing unlike any before, a colossal gateway materialized—an archway adorned with symbols representing the myriad paths of humanity. Beyond it, a boundless expanse of light beckoned.

Chantry and Ethan exchanged a glance, their hands entwined. "What lies beyond?" Ethan wondered aloud.

The crow, perched on the archway, spoke with enigmatic certainty. "The culmination of love, the convergence of destinies, and the revelation of a cosmic truth."

With hesitant yet resolute steps, they crossed the threshold. The world beneath them blurred, and the cosmic tapestry unfolded, revealing connections spanning across epochs. Voices from the past, present, and future echoed, creating a symphony that transcended time.

And then, in a crescendo of brilliance, the universe held its breath. Chantry and Ethan stood at the precipice of something extraordinary—a revelation that promised to redefine their understanding of existence.

As the final notes of the cosmic symphony echoed, the story hung in the balance, poised on the edge of a revelation that could reshape the very fabric of reality.

The tale of Chantry and Ethan, the journey of the invisible staircases, reached an ephemeral juncture—a cliffhanger suspended between the known and the unknown. The world, enraptured by their saga, awaited the unveiling of the mysteries that lingered in the celestial expanse beyond.

Made in the USA
Columbia, SC
19 June 2024